HOOK'S DAUGHTER
THE UNTOLD TALE OF A PIRATE PRINCESS

THE PIRATE PRINCESS CHRONICLES

R. V. BOWMAN

In Loving Memory of My Dad
Who never stopped being my hero
F. Rodney McColm
(Dec. 24, 1938 - Sept. 6, 2017)

CONTENTS

AUTHOR'S NOTE

This book is a derivative work loosely based off of *Peter and Wendy*, a novel by J.M. Barrie. Peter Pan first appeared as a seven-day-old baby in a chapter of his novel *The Little White Bird*, published in 1902. The Peter Pan most people know is from a play written by Barrie and then performed on stage in 1904 called *Peter Pan, or The Boy Who Never Grew Up*. The play was later adapted into the above mentioned novel in 1911. The story has since seen many adaptations, including the well-known Disney film *Peter Pan*.

Since the beginning of this book is set in the North London suburb of Tottenham during the Edwardian period, I did quite a bit of research into that time period, including what people wore, what they ate, and how they spoke. Some of the terms, such as *balmy on the crumpet*, that were used in this book were commonplace slang of the time period.

One of my biggest challenges while planning the action of this book was figuring out how to get Rommy from Tottenham to the Victorian Docks, a journey which would have been next to impossible for a young, upper class girl to make unchaperoned during that time period. In order to do that, I had to fudge history just a little bit. The best and easiest way to get Rommy over the distance she needed to travel was to use the London Underground or Tube Station. Trying to find which rail line was added when and to where involved a bit of digging. It turned out there was a railway line that did bring workers from Tottenham into Central London and even offered access to the ports of London where the Victoria Docks were located. However, these were all above ground trains, even though they were still often called the Tube Station or the Underground. A direct underground route from Tottenham to the Victoria Docks wasn't installed until the 1960s.

Besides Peter Pan, Captain Hook and Neverland, all featured in Barrie's novel, the people and places in this book are completely of my own imagination. Chattingham's School for Modern Girls has never existed to my knowledge. However, the place I chose for the school was loosely based on an actual school that existed and was housed in Bruce Castle in Tottenham from 1827 to 1891. That school was for boys, but, like Chattingham's was very progressive for the time period. Bruce Castle is now Bruce Castle Museum and is open to the public.

I

THE DUEL

Tottenham, England
April 1910

"Andromeda Cavendish's dueling partner will be..." Miss Watson put her hand into the velvet bag and pulled out the marker. "Primrose Beechwood."

Rommy's hand tightened reflexively on the hilt of her fencing sword. Taking a deep breath, she pushed to her feet.

On the opposite side of the room, a tall, golden-haired girl stood up from the fencing team's bench. Girls on both sides of the room clapped and cheered. Rommy heard someone give a whoop, and she smiled. It had to be Francie.

Miss Watson cleared her throat. "This duel is the last of the three challenging matches. If won,

Andromeda will earn a place on the Chattingham Girls' Varsity Fencing Team. The official regulations for duels will apply. The winner of this match will be the first duelist to reach 10 points. Please take your places."

Rommy's stomach swooped with nerves, and she clenched her sword tighter. She and Primrose stepped onto opposite edges of the dueling mat and faced each other.

Rommy drew her thin-bladed sword up to salute her opponent with a trembling hand. Across from her, Primrose did the same, adding a fancy flourish to the end of hers. The two girls then faced and saluted Miss Watson, the director of the match, and then Mrs. Wilkes, Miss Bludge and Monsieur Bouvier, the three judges. The judges smiled and nodded as Rommy and Primrose again faced each other.

"*En garde,*" said Miss Watson.

Rommy and Primrose slid on their masks and held up their swords in the ready stance. Primrose's smirk was visible through the screen of her visor. Rommy lifted her chin and pressed her lips together. Primrose had the advantage of being a head taller than she was, but Rommy had been watching Primrose for the last year. She favored going to the right, and she was slower than Rommy who was small and quick. She could dance under someone's guard and, before her opponent even knew what she was about, strike a touch.

"*Pret,*" Miss Watson said.

Rommy tensed, ready to lunge forward to get a first touch and the first point of the match.

"*Allez.*"

Rommy didn't hesitate. She closed the gap between herself and Primrose and lunged under her left side.

"Touch."

Rommy and Primrose stepped back and got into the ready position again.

"*Allez,*" Miss Watson called.

This time, Primrose attacked first, lunging forward. Rommy blocked her thrust and countered with a lunge of her own under Primrose's left side again.

"Touch," rang out again. Rommy had her second point. Only eight more to go.

The next point went to Primrose who used her long reach to hit Rommy squarely in the chest. Despite the padded jacket she wore, Rommy knew she'd have a bruise in the morning.

Back and forth, the two girls attacked and defended and counter-attacked. At the end of the first three-minute period, Rommy was ahead four to three.

Miss Watson called for the one minute break. Rommy retreated to her bench and used her hand-kerchief to mop her face. She took a long drink from her water flask.

The break seemed to last hardly a moment before Miss Watson called the girls back to the dueling mat.

Again the two girls' feet danced across the mat, lunging, striking, and parrying. The cheers from the other students were muted in Rommy's ears. Her sole focus was Primrose, trying to read the other girl before she moved. Rommy knew her quickness was her only chance to win. Primrose was older and larger. If it came down to strength, Rommy knew she'd lose.

The second three-minute period ended. This time, Primrose led, eight to seven. As the two readied themselves again, Primrose's eyes bored into her own. A smile, more like a grimace, graced the girl's face under her mask. Rommy's confidence slipped. Primrose only needed two more points, and Rommy was tired. She shook her head and squared her shoulders. She could do this.

"*Allez*," called Miss Watson.

Rommy lunged forward, feinting to the left. As Primrose moved to defend the attack, Rommy flicked her sword under her opponent's.

"Touch."

Tied. Only two more points.

When Miss Watson called *allez* again, Primrose went on the attack. She moved Rommy back with a flurry of sword strikes while Rommy desperately parried each blow. The capped tip of Primrose's blade dug into Rommy's sword arm, and she sucked in her breath as pain streaked up her arm.

"Fault," said Miss Watson. "Duelist Primrose, please strike only in the approved target areas. *En garde.*"

Primrose and Rommy again took their ready positions.

"*Pret.*"

Rommy tensed even as her sword arm throbbed. Quick. She had to get in quick before Primrose could press the advantage of her injury.

"*Allez.*"

Rommy darted forward and feinted right. Primrose, wise to Rommy's move, parried. They danced forward and back, each trying to gain the advantage. Rommy whipped her sword around to the side, striking Primrose's left hip. It was on the edge of the allowed target area. She breathed a sigh of relief when Miss Watson said, "Touch."

Just one more point. One more point and then, maybe, her father would take her to sea with him this summer. She needed to prove she could defend herself. She would overcome any of his excuses if she could just make the team, if she could show him she was tougher than he thought. That she wasn't her mother.

The two girls came together again in a clash of swords. Rommy could see the sheen of rage in Primrose's eyes. Primrose hated losing and worse, losing face among the other girls. She was 14, and Rommy was just 12. Today.

Primrose's sword came down in a vicious swipe. At the last second Rommy blocked it, but Primrose, with all of her height, was bearing down on Rommy. Gripping her sword with both hands, Rommy held Primrose's downward thrust, but just barely. New sweat beaded on her forehead, and her arms shook. Her injured arm throbbed. She had to do something.

The new technique Monsieur Bouvier had taught her last week flashed into her mind, but she had only practiced it a few times.

Primrose pressed down harder, and Rommy knew her arms wouldn't hold much longer. Taking a deep breath, she swirled away from and behind her opponent. Rommy extended her arm behind her, striking Primrose's shoulder.

"Touch! That is the tenth point. Duelist Andromeda Cavendish has won the point and the match," announced Miss Watson.

The students erupted into cheers. A few stamped their feet on the bleachers, and there were a few whoops and whistles heard above the general noise.

Primrose ripped off her mask. "Miss Watson, she hit me from the back. Surely, that is not ladylike conduct in a match."

Miss Watson hesitated. Monsieur Bouvier stood. "They call the counter riposte that Miss Cavendish used the black diamond, which is indeed an accepted strike on the dueling mat. I would also like to note it is not ladylike conduct to lunge downward on an opponent half your size, Miss Beechwood. Touches to the head do not count in any case. Accept your loss graciously and be happy that you now have such an accomplished teammate."

Rommy approached the middle of the mat and saluted Primrose who saluted back. The two shook hands, and Primrose squeezed Rommy's hand until the bones crunched together. She pulled Rommy in closer.

"Don't get too comfortable on the team," she said.

2

THE HOPE

"All right, ladies," said Miss Watson, clapping her hands to get everyone's attention. "Afternoon tea is in one hour. Please be punctual. You are dismissed."

She walked over to the bench where Rommy was gathering her things. "Andromeda, your father should arrive around teatime, so you are excused to go right to the visiting parlor." Miss Watson put her hand on Rommy's shoulder. "Congratulations. You did well."

Rommy ducked her head. "Thank you, Miss Watson," she said.

Miss Watson turned to leave just as Francie, Rommy's roommate and best friend, came charging across the floor.

"You did it, Rommy. The youngest member. It's so marvelous. Aren't you excited?" Francie latched onto

Rommy's arm and leaned in closer. "And did you see Primrose's face?"

"I could hardly miss her glaring at me," Rommy said. "I still can't quite believe it." She shook her head as the two walked from the exercise room and out into the hallway. "I only hope it's enough to convince Papa."

"I don't see how your father could say no," said Francie. "You were wonderful."

Rommy made a face. "I don't think Primrose agrees. She certainly won't be welcoming me onto the team with the hand of friendship."

"Don't be silly, Rommy. Of course Primrose isn't happy," said Francie as the two girls made their way up the big central staircase toward their rooms on the third floor. "You defeated her in front of half the school, and she's two full years ahead of you. You know how her family is, too. Her father will likely humiliate her for losing."

By the time the girls had made their way to their corner suite, Francie was out of breath. One of the bigger rooms, it sported a spacious bedroom, large windows and a separate sitting nook. With her mother dead and her father out at sea most of the time, Rommy had been staying year round at Chattingham's since she had arrived seven years ago. That is, until Francie's arrival three years ago. Now, Rommy often spent school holidays with Francie's family, but the corner suite remained theirs.

Rommy looked around the room. It was the only home she remembered. She had vague recollections of a big brownstone with heavy, dark furniture, but the memories had faded over the years. Now she wasn't sure if the things she remembered were real or something she had dreamed.

"I thought you were done for there at the end." Francie danced across the floor, her voice pulling Rommy away from her thoughts. "Then, whoosh, you twirled and whirled. It was just like you were dancing, Rommy."

With a final pirouette, Francie flopped backwards onto the bed and giggled. Her black curls spilled over the far side of the bed. She suddenly sat straight up. "Which dress will you wear tonight? You want to look elegant, so your father can see how mature you are."

"I don't know, Francie. I want to look strong, not elegant."

"Well, silly, you can't wear your fencing garb to the visiting parlor. What would Mrs. Blakely think?" Francie's dark eyes sparkled at the idea of the very proper etiquette instructor's expression if Rommy went into the formal parlor in her fencing outfit.

A laugh spurted out of Rommy. "No, Mrs. Blakely definitely would not approve!"

"I think you should wear the blue with the scalloped lace trim and your white kid slippers. It makes you look much more grown up. Do you want me to help you braid your hair up high? Everyone would be scandalized if you wore it up, but a high braid won't be amiss."

Francie bounced up and gathered her things to help Rommy get ready. Rommy stood at the wash basin in her chemise and washed up as best she could. She patted her face dry and then spun to face her friend.

"Oh, Francie, I'm so nervous. What if Papa says no?" A stinging started behind her eyes, but she blinked back the tears. Rommy rarely cried. After all, what good did it do? "I have to spend the summer with Papa. I can't even think about him saying no."

"You know you are always welcome at Hyde House," said Francie. She came over to stand by Rommy, slinging an arm around her shoulders. "Mama loves having you. She says you have a wonderfully civilizing effect on me."

"And I love your family, Francie, truly I do, but I miss Papa so much. I only see him two days out of the whole year, and it's just not enough. I feel like we don't even know each other."

Rommy dropped the hand towel she'd been twisting and squared her shoulders. "He has to let me go. Nobody has ever made the Chattingham Girls' Varsity Fencing Team at 12. He'll have to admit that I am strong and can take care of myself." Her hands tightened into fists. "I'll make him see."

"Well, he won't see anything if you don't get

ready," said Francie, pushing Rommy into the chair in front of the mirror. "Plus, I can't wait to see Primrose's face at tea. It will be so much fun watching her try to act like she doesn't care she lost."

"Francie, you enjoy tormenting Primrose too much." Rommy twisted in the chair to admonish her friend.

Francie pushed her back around. "Don't act all prim and proper. You know she's been absolutely horrid to you since she started attending Chattingham's. She's bound to be positively unbearable now." Francie rolled her eyes as she brushed Rommy's thick, tawny hair.

"I still don't know why she's never liked me, but I'm sure she positively loathes me now," Rommy said, letting out a sigh.

"She's just jealous. She took an instant dislike to you after your father came to visit with a stack of new frocks, that lovely locket, and a pile of pin money." While she talked, Francie's fingers flew as she twisted Rommy's hair into an intricate braid high on the back of her head. "It didn't help you witnessed that horrible scene her father made in the parlor about her mid-finals."

"It was hard not to hear with him shouting like that," said Rommy. "I tried to slip away, but then I knocked over that dumb door stop. When I remember all the nasty things he said to her, I feel sorry for Primrose."

"Don't forget, your father has a title, too, even if he is a second son," said Francie. "Poor Primrose. Her father is positively filthy rich, but it all came from trade. And he's such a miser. She hardly has any pin money to spend. Mother says it's a positive disgrace, and his disposition is so sour it would curdle milk."

"Francie! I can't believe you said that!" said Rommy.

"What? You know it's true." Francie shrugged. "Still, I do feel sorry for Primrose at times, but she is so horrid to you, I can't like her."

Rommy turned and hugged Francie around the waist. "You are the best friend."

"Don't get all sentimental. Now, turn around, so I can finish your hair. We have to make you look mature and ready for anything, so your father will say yes." Francie grinned at Rommy in the mirror. "I know he will, Rommy. This is the year!"

3
THE VISIT

Rommy looked at the clock again. It had been just over an hour since Francie had squeezed her hand and wished her luck, and Papa still wasn't here. She got up and stood by the window of the visiting parlor. The draperies were parted, and the late afternoon sun had given way to early twilight.

To pass the time, Rommy went over her arguments again to convince Papa to take her with him this summer. She was halfway through her list when something brushed against her ankle. Miss Cleopatra, the resident cat, had meandered into the room. Now she wound around Rommy's ankles purring. Rommy stooped and gathered the cat up in her arms.

"I wonder why Papa's so late," she said to the cat. The cat simply butted her head against Rommy's chin, her polite way of asking to be petted.

Rommy obliged, rubbing the cat behind her tufted ears.

Suddenly, the cat tensed and stared out the window. She let out a soft hiss. Rommy peered out, too. With the sunshine gone, there were only gray shadows outside. She held Miss Cleo close as she gazed into the gloom gathered beneath the trees. The branches of the large chestnut tree swayed as if something had recently left their boughs. Was that a shadow? Rommy squinted but could see nothing. She shook her head.

"Silly cat. Did you see another cat or perhaps a squirrel? Whatever it was, it's gone now."

Rommy gave a last glance and returned to her chair. The clock chimed six o'clock. She had barely settled herself and the cat when a familiar voice made both her and Miss Cleo tense up again.

"I see you are still waiting," said Primrose who stood in the doorway of the parlor with Lily and Violet. Francie always called them the wilting bouquet.

The thought made Rommy smile, and she lifted her chin. The only way to survive an attack by Primrose was to act like she didn't care in the least, no matter what the girl said. Rommy knew Primrose would be even more unpleasant after losing this afternoon. "Something delayed Papa. It's not unusual in his line of work."

"Delayed? You'd assume that since he only gets to

see his precious daughter for a few hours two days a year, he wouldn't want to be late by so much as a moment." Lily and Violet giggled on cue. "But then, maybe he doesn't want to make the most of every moment. Maybe he doesn't care at all."

Rommy knew better than to respond. Her words would only be twisted into an argument she couldn't win. Not with her father still absent, anyway.

A clear voice came from outside the parlor. "Primrose, Lily, Violet? Shouldn't you girls be in the music room for your lessons?" Miss Watson stood in the hallway. "It's sweet of you girls to check on Andromeda, but you really must not be late to your lessons. Mr. Montclair is waiting, and his time is very precious."

"Yes, Miss Watson," the three girls chorused, but not before Primrose had shot Rommy a narrow-eyed glare that promised more ugliness when a teacher wasn't around. Rommy breathed a small inward sigh. She wasn't afraid of Primrose, precisely, but she tried to avoid these encounters. Being on the fencing team with the girl would make that much more difficult.

"Andromeda, do you want me to have Mrs. Stackhouse send up tea? I'm sure your father will be here soon." Miss Watson smiled kindly.

"Yes, ma'am, that would be wonderful. Papa will be famished when he gets here. I'm sure he was just delayed along the way."

"I'm sure," said her teacher and turned away to go to the kitchens.

It took forty-five minutes for the tea to arrive. Miss Watson brought it herself. She placed it on the low coffee table and took a seat in the chair across from Rommy. By this time it was after 7 p.m.

"Andromeda, dear, can I pour for you?"

"Oh no, I want to wait for Papa," said Rommy, although her stomach had been steadily sinking since the clock had chimed 6:30. Papa was never this late, at least not without sending word. Rommy shuddered, remembering the only other time he had been delayed this long.

"Andromeda."

Rommy looked up at Miss Watson; her blue eyes were kind. "I think we probably have to face the fact your father is not coming tonight."

"But.."

The woman held up her hand to forestall Rommy's protests. "I realize it is a great disappointment and that you look forward to these visits, but if your father was coming and just delayed, he would have sent word by now. I think we are going to have to accept that he isn't coming today. I understand this is not the present you wanted on your birthday." She reached out and patted Rommy's hand. "I did have Mrs. Stackhouse add a small coconut cake. I know they are your favorite. Why don't we have our tea and then you can go back up to your rooms. I won't make you go to the end of music lessons tonight since you've already missed most of them."

Rommy's shoulders slumped, but she dutifully placed Miss Cleo on the floor. "Thank you. You are very kind," she choked out.

Her teacher poured the tea and handed a cup to Rommy. The cup clattered in the saucer but Rommy managed not to spill it. She picked up the coconut cake and swallowed a few bites. Each one stuck in her throat. She blinked to keep the tears from spilling over. She just wanted to go to her room. The day had held such promise. Her win seemed like a sign things would be different. It only made her disappointment that much worse.

Miss Watson had picked up a dainty watercress sandwich. She paused when Rommy's lip quivered. "Oh Andromeda, I appreciate you are dreadfully disappointed, but I'm positive there is an explanation. Shipping is always unreliable. It's a wonder that your father hasn't missed one of these visits before now. After all," she said with a smile, "even the great Captain Cavendish cannot control the weather."

Rommy tried to return the smile, but couldn't quite manage it. "What if he doesn't come at all? I so wanted to tell him I made the fencing team."

Miss Watson leaned forward. "He will be so proud of you, Andromeda. I know that I am. You worked hard and achieved something nobody at Chattingham's has ever done before. That's quite noteworthy." She smiled. "I'm sure he'll be here within a day or two. Your father loves you, and this separation is likely as painful for him as it is for you."

Rommy couldn't help the question that burst from her lips or the hope attached to the answer. "Do you think so?"

"Yes, my dear, I do. Now why don't you run along upstairs. I'm sure Francie will help you find your smile again. I'll take care of the tea things." Miss Watson stood, and Rommy did, too.

Rommy turned to go and then stopped. "Thank you, Miss Watson, for the tea... and things. Let Mrs. Stackhouse know that her coconut cake was most delicious."

Miss Watson smiled, but it didn't quite reach her eyes.

4
THE IDEA

Rommy was on the second landing of the staircase headed to her room when she heard Primrose's voice again. "Oh, Andromeda," said Primrose. "I'm so sorry your father didn't make it. How sad for you." Following behind her, Violet and Lily giggled.

Primrose came up and dropped her arm around Rommy's shoulders. Rommy shrugged her off and continued up the stairs. If she could just get to her room, she could lock Primrose and her friends out.

"Maybe he got busy and forgot."

Obviously, Primrose wasn't going to give up.

Rommy shrugged again and continued moving. She figured the less she said, the better.

"Or maybe your father had something better to do than to see his daughter. Christmas is only, let's see," Primrose paused on the stairway, "a little over seven months away. You'd think he would have at least let you know he wasn't coming instead of letting you sit in the parlor all evening."

"I'm sure he would have if he could." Rommy couldn't help the words from tumbling out.

"It's so humiliating to be stood up by one's own father." Primrose shook her head. The other two girls giggled again.

They had made it to the third floor. Rommy smiled tightly and headed toward her room at the far end of the hallway, but Primrose blocked her path. Lily stood on one side and Violet on the other.

Placing a hand to her mouth in exaggerated concern, Primrose said, "Oh dear, I hope nothing has happened to him. The oceans are so terribly dangerous."

Rommy couldn't help the quick intake of breath. Primrose seeing her advantage leaped on the vulnerability. "Shipwrecked or drowned in a storm, or attacked by pirates and made to walk the plank - who knows what's really happened. You must be so worried. I can't imagine what other reason would keep him from letting you know he would be late."

Lily put her hand on Primrose's arm. "Primrose, you shouldn't…" Primrose pulled her arm away and gave Rommy a nasty smile.

A stinging sensation began behind Rommy's eyes, and she swallowed to keep the tears at bay. If she could just get in her room.

"It's really too bad he isn't here." Primrose sighed. "I guess it's another summer here at school. Maybe Francie's family will take pity on you again and let you come home with her. I'm sure her family is kind enough not to mind the imposition."

"My mother adores Rommy, and we'd be oh so lucky to have her with us this summer," a bright voice said behind them. Francie shouldered her way to stand next to Rommy and gave Primrose a pointed look. "Unfortunately for you, you'll be spending the entire summer with your father."

Primrose sniffed. "I'm sure I don't know what you mean."

Francie pressed her advantage. "Just think, an entire summer of listening to all the ways your father expects you to improve." She cocked her head. "With his wise tutelage, I'm sure you'll finally bring up those French scores." Francie gave a savage grin.

"You are a rude and uncouth girl, Frances Hyde." Primrose pushed through both girls and walked stiffly down the hallway, Lily and Violet trailing behind her.

"Don't you think you were a bit harsh?" said Rommy as she watched Primrose walk away.

"Would you rather stand there and be target practice for her?" Francie retorted. "No, you should be saying, 'Thank you, Francie, for saving me from the vile clutches of Primrose Beechwood. I am forever in your debt and will give you my firstborn as payment, or better yet, take you with me on my father's ship this summer'."

"I don't even know if *I'll* be on Papa's ship this summer," Rommy said, her gloomy mood returning as the two girls entered their room. "What if something genuinely has happened to him? I can't believe he wouldn't send word if he was only delayed."

"You worry too much, Rommy." Francie collapsed onto her bed and pulled Rommy down with her.

"Francie, the last time my father was this late, he arrived with a silver hook instead of a hand."

Francie wrinkled her nose. "Well, there is that, but he was otherwise fine. Did he ever tell you what happened?"

"No, not with any detail. What if he doesn't come at all? What if he's in trouble?" Rommy felt tears stinging her eyes again. She rubbed at them impatiently. She hated crying, and it felt like tears had been threatening all day.

"What can you do if he is?" said Francie flopping onto her back. "You can't go sailing the seven seas looking for him. He could be anywhere. He most likely got tied up in some port or another. You know how these foreign places are. Most have miles and miles of paperwork."

"I wish there was some way I could get word to his offices. Perhaps someone down there would know something." Rommy put her hands over her face. "He has to come before we get out for summer holidays. You know I love your family, but I couldn't bear the disappointment if I don't get to spend this summer with him."

Francie sat straight up on the bed. "That's it!" She bounced up and paced the confines of their bedroom. "You could go down to the docks where his office is. Someone down there might have learned something or that clerk of his - what's his name - he'd know something."

"Are you insane? There is no way that Mrs. Wilkes will let me go down to the docks. Who would chaperone me?"

"Are you balmy on the crumpet? You wouldn't tell anyone!" Francie put her hands on her hips and rolled her eyes. "Sometimes, Rommy, you are too concerned with the rules. Do you want to find out what happened to your father or not?"

"Balmy on the crumpet? What does that even mean? If your mother found out you were using slang, she would be livid."

Francie let out a snort of laughter. "Mother would swoon. Charlie taught me that one," she said referring to her second oldest brother, one of her seven siblings. "It means you are not right in the head, and stop trying to change the subject."

"I can't just sneak out of Chattingham's. I'd get in so much trouble if I got caught. I'd likely get kicked off the fencing team and then where would I be when Papa shows up?"

"At least he would know you could take initiative," said Francie. "Where has all that rule following gotten you anyhow?"

Rommy threw up her hands. "A lone girl can't go wandering around the docks. I wouldn't make it past the Tube Station before someone would return me to the school's front doorstep!" By this time Rommy too was standing and her voice had risen.

"Sshhh - do you want everyone to hear you?" Francie grabbed Rommy's hands and pulled her back down to sit on the bed. "You could sneak out, and I'd cover for you. It wouldn't take more than a day, and then you could sneak back in when it got dark again. If you dress in your fencing outfit and stuff your hair up under a cap, you could pass for a boy."

"Thanks loads," said Rommy, letting out a strangled laugh. "I guess being so small is finally coming in handy."

"It could definitely work," said Francie. Her eyes were shining with excitement.

"I don't know, Francie," said Rommy. "I don't know how we could possibly pull this off without getting caught, and what would I do if they kicked me out of school? I have nowhere to go. Even our house in town has only a skeleton crew of servants. And if Papa came back, he'd be furious."

"You won't get caught. I have some experience in

fooling adults," said Francie. "And even if you do get caught, I bet if you cry and tell them how worried you are about your father, Mrs. Wilkes wouldn't be so heartless as to throw you out. You might get punished, but I will lay odds they won't even kick you off the fencing team."

"I don't know," Rommy said. "Maybe I'll hear from Papa in the morning."

"Just think, Rommy. Actually doing something rather than waiting around for an answer. That will surely impress your father with your resourcefulness. What better way to prove that you can go with your father when he finally shows up?"

Rommy bit her lip. "It's an awfully big risk. If we get caught…"

Francie stood up and shrugged. "If it was me, I don't think I could just sit around and wait, but it's up to you." She gave an exaggerated yawn. "If we aren't going to plot your escape, I'm going to bed."

"I didn't say it wasn't a good idea, but what if he shows up tomorrow? I think waiting to see if Papa turns up is the sensible thing to do."

Francie quirked an eyebrow. "And we know you always do the sensible thing."

Stung, Rommie turned away. She slipped her shoes off and started to unbutton her dress. Silence stretched between the two girls. Francie was the first to break it, throwing her arms around Rommy in an impulsive hug. "I'm sorry. I just got so excited about planning a great escape. You are likely right, and you'll hear from him in the morning."

The tension in Rommy's shoulders drained away as she hugged Francie back. "It's a good idea, but there's no use planning anything if Papa shows up."

"You're right," said Francie. "We'll see what tomorrow brings."

The two girls got into their night clothes, cleaned their teeth, and climbed into bed. Francie turned down the gas lamp, and soon Rommy could hear her soft breathing that signaled she had fallen asleep.

It took Rommy a considerably longer time to find sleep.

5
THE DECISION

The next morning, Rommy and Francie headed into the breakfast room which was already full of students. While the teachers encouraged the girls to use good manners and not be coarsely loud, it was also a time they could socialize. The room held a pleasant hum of conversation accented by the clink of silverware.

After loading up their plates from the tantalizing array of foods on the large sideboard, the girls made their way to a table in the far corner. Several of their classmates had saved them seats, since they were, as usual, some of the last to arrive for breakfast. Francie hated getting up in the morning.

"Congratulations, Rommy!" said Eleanore. "I have to say, it was absolutely brilliant how you won that last match. Especially against Primrose."

Adelaide nodded, her glasses sliding down her nose. "*Especially* against Primrose."

The girls all exchanged looks. Primrose was less than popular with the younger girls as she took every opportunity to humiliate them. She never pulled that with the girls her age or older, but the younger students were always targets for her. They all resented it.

"Thank you," Rommy said, ducking her head. "Primrose was a very difficult opponent. Either of us could have won. It was as much luck as skill."

"Luck?" Francie scoffed. "Rommy, you are one of the best fencers at the school and now everyone knows it. Especially Primrose Beechwood!"

Laughing, the other girls agreed with Francie's enthusiastic pronouncement.

The conversation moved on to the upcoming dance that Worthington Young Men's Academy, their brother school, would be hosting. As second years, they weren't allowed to take part in dances until next year.

This did not stop the girls from chattering about the dresses the older girls would be wearing and which boys would dance with whom. Rommy let the conversation flow around her, as she looked around for Miss Watson. She waited all through breakfast for a message from her father but none came. The food that had looked so good only a short while ago, tasted like sawdust. Rommy pushed back her half-finished plate.

As the girls got up from the table, Francie hooked her arm through Rommy's. "Why don't you go find one of the teachers and ask if you have any messages? I'll bring your books and notebook to mathematics. You can meet me there."

Rommy squeezed Francie's hand and smiled at her. "Thanks!"

Rommy hurried from the breakfast room to Miss Watson's classroom where she knew the woman would be preparing for her first year literature students. When Rommy entered the room, her teacher was writing a Tennyson poem on her black board.

"Miss Watson?" Rommy said.

"Oh, Andromeda." Miss Watson swung around. "You startled me. What did you need, dear? Don't you have class soon?"

"Yes, ma'am, but I wanted to ask.. .That is… I was wondering if there had been any message from my father." Rommy tried to keep the desperation out of her voice. She must not have done as good of a job as she thought though. Miss Watson set down her chalk and came to stand in front of Rommy, a look of sympathy on her face.

"No, I'm sorry. There has been no word, Andromeda, but I don't want you to worry. It's not unusual for ships to get to port late, and messages are not always reliable. Your father is an excellent seaman with a seaworthy vessel, and I'm sure he will send word just as soon as he can."

Rommy swallowed down her disappointment. "Thank you. I'm sure you are right."

She turned to go.

"Andromeda?"

Rommy turned back around. "Yes?"

"If any word comes, I will get it to you right away. I know waiting is difficult." Miss Watson smiled at her.

"Thank you. I appreciate that."

Rommy hurried from the room and headed to her mathematics class. It was her least favorite class, but at least Miss Bludge was nice.

She slipped into her desk next to Francie. The teacher nodded to her and continued to write the days' problems on the board. Francie leaned over.

"I can tell by your face—you didn't hear anything did you?"

Rommy shook her head, afraid to speak lest her voice give away how upset she was.

Francie made a sympathetic face and opened her mouth to say something, but Miss Bludge clapped her hands.

"All right, class," Miss Bludge said in her high, trilling voice. "Today we will work on long division.

Please copy down and work out the following problems. We'll be sharing our answers and how we got them on the board in a little while."

Rommy was glad for the distraction. She loved Francie, and she knew her friend meant well, but, Rommy didn't want to hear any more well-meaning assurances that nobody believed anyway.

She bent over her work, trying to concentrate on the numbers, but her father's absence was too big to push away.

The hour dragged on as Miss Bludge called the girls one by one up to the board to show how they got their answers. With each moment that ticked by, Rommy felt her frustration build. She was relieved when the clock chimed the top of the hour, announcing that class was over. Rommy had made a decision, and she couldn't wait to tell her friend.

Hooking her arm with Francie's, she pulled her out into the hallway.

Leaning in close, she said, "I'm doing it. I'm going to Papa's offices."

Francie stopped and spun toward her. "Truly?" she said, her eyes big as she practically bounced in place. Students going to their next classes had to detour around them.

"Sshh," said Rommy, grabbing Francie's arm again and pulling her along. "I don't want everyone to hear us."

Francie lowered her voice, but her whole body

vibrated with excitement. "We need to plan as soon as possible. Let's sit on our own at lunch so we can get started."

Rommy nodded in agreement. She couldn't help the grin that tugged at her mouth.

6

THE RIVAL

When Rommy hurried into the lunchroom after French class, she spotted Francie's black curls on the far side of the room. As she made her way to the sideboard where the luncheon was laid out, she caught some girls giving her sympathetic looks. Apparently, her father's absence had circulated. She could guess who had shared that information.

Francie looked up from a piece of paper she was writing on when Rommy reached the table juggling her satchel and her tray of food.

"How did you get this table to yourself?" Rommy asked, sitting down. It was one of the smaller tables, but usually they sat with several of the other second years.

Francie made a face. "I hope you won't be mad, but I used your father's absence as an excuse." Before

Rommy could answer, she rushed on, "A lot of people already knew."

Rommy felt a spurt of annoyance. She hated the feeling that everyone knew her business and felt sorry for her, but the hesitant look on Francie's face made her shove that annoyance to the side. Francie was only trying to help. "It's all right," she said. "I don't much like everyone feeling sorry for me, but it would be hard to talk about this with anyone else around."

Francie smiled. "I knew you'd understand." She turned the paper around so Rommy could see it. "I have the perfect plan. I made an excuse to go into the kitchens when I got here, and I found out from Mrs. Stackhouse that the milkman comes every morning at about 5 a.m."

"What's the milkman got to do with me leaving Chattingham's?" Rommy asked, puzzled.

"We're his last stop," said Francie, bouncing in her seat. "After he drops off our milk, he heads back through the center of Tottenham because Milligan's Dairy is on the far side of town."

"So, that means what, exactly?" said Rommy.

"It means the railway station is downtown, and the milkman goes right by it," Francie said.

Rommy was leaning in closer to see the small map Francie was sketching when a voice spoke loud enough for everyone at the adjacent tables to hear.

"What are you two doing here all by yourselves?"

Francie and Rommy looked up to see Primrose, with Violet and Lily in tow, heading their way. Francie pushed the paper she'd been writing on underneath her plate as the three made their way to the table.

"What do you want, Primrose?" Francie said.

"You two looked so lonely over here. What happened, did your little friends tire of you?" Violet and Lily giggled. Rommy wondered if either of them ever thought for themselves or if they always followed Primrose's lead.

A mean glint came into Primrose's eyes. "Or did you need to come over here to have a little cry because your dearest papa hasn't shown up yet?"

"Your concern is touching," said Rommy through gritted teeth, "but I'm just fine."

"No need to put on a brave front, Andromeda." Seeing Rommy's expression, she smirked. "What's the matter? Afraid he's not truly delayed and that you aren't important enough for him to come see you?"

Rommy deliberately turned her back and took a large bite out her sandwich. Perhaps Primrose would get the hint.

She didn't.

"Presents and money don't mean your father

loves you. It just means he thinks he can buy you," Primrose said, leaning toward her.

Francie pushed to her feet. "The problem with you, Primrose, is that you think anyone cares what you believe."

"More people care than you realize, Frances Hyde," retorted Primrose. "And I bet they'd be terribly interested to learn what I know about your little secret." Her hand darted out and snagged the corner of the paper under Francie's plate.

Dread pooled in Rommy's stomach.

Primrose held the paper between two fingers like it was contaminated. "What have we here? A map of some kind." She sneered at Francie. "Now what would you and Andromeda need with a map marking the entrance of the Underground? I will lay odds that Mrs. Wilkes would be interested to learn that. Imagine, her precious Andromeda and Frances up to no good. Whatever will she say?"

Primrose's smile held the smug satisfaction of knowing she had the upper hand.

Rage and panic fought for first place as Rommy's hands curled into fists. She had done nothing to Primrose, but that didn't stop her from taking every opportunity to make Rommy's life difficult. It wasn't fair. Primrose was not going to ruin her plans to find her papa. The lunchroom faded away, and the noise became a distant buzz. All she could hear was a pounding in her ears. She shoved up from her chair, her arm seeming to pull back by itself. Primrose's pale eyes widened, and she took a step back. Then Francie's hand was on Rommy's shoulder and her cool, amused voice broke through the red haze. The lunchroom and all its noise came rushing back. Rommy sat down hard, her arms and legs trembling. Had she really almost hit Primrose?

"Oh, Primrose," Francie said as Rommy's attention snapped back into focus. "I'm sure you don't understand this, but my parents are coming to take Rommy and me on a little outing. You know, a trip into town for ices and a few treats and trinkets. But then, your father wouldn't do that, would he? After all, that would cost money."

Rommy stared in fascination as a mottled purplish color spread up from the neck of Primrose's uniform to her hairline. She was trying to speak, but nothing but hisses of air were coming through her lips. Francie leaned forwarded and plucked the paper out of Primrose's hand.

"Come on, Rommy," said Francie. "Grab your sandwich and let's go to our room. It appears you can't even have a private conversation without rude interruptions."

Rommy grabbed her food and satchel and followed Francie out of the room. When she looked back, Primrose was still purple-faced and sputtering.

7

THE PLAN

Francie flung open the door to their room, making it bang against the wall. Her coolness had disappeared once they had cleared the lunchroom. "That Primrose is a complete git and full of tosh."

Rommy snorted. "If by that you mean nasty and mean, I have to agree with you."

Francie shrugged her shoulders. "Close enough." Then she grinned. "I can't believe you almost hit Primrose!"

Rommy shook her head. "I can't either. It would have ruined our plans if I had though."

"I don't know," said Francie, a burst of laughter escaping. "It would have been almost worth it to see you punch Primrose right in her mean little mouth. Did you see the way she backed away from you?"

The smile on Rommy's face slid away. "I don't

know, Francie. I think it might have hurt less if I had hit her. I don't think I've ever seen her so angry or upset."

Francie gave Rommy's shoulder a friendly push. "Knock it off."

"Knock off what?" Rommy asked.

"I can hear it in your voice," said Francie. "You feel sorry for her. You should save your sympathy for someone who deserves it."

Rommy shrugged. "I just know how I feel when she twits me about Papa. It hurts because some of it is true. He isn't here very much, and sometimes, well, sometimes I just don't feel like I matter that much to him."

Francie stared at her for a moment and then went off into a peal of laughter. "Oh, Rommy! You can't really believe you don't matter to your father. This is the same man who brought you a pearl locket from an oyster he found himself. He showers you with gifts and obviously adores you when he is here. Not to mention, your father is dashing and has grand adventures and makes all the other fathers, especially Primrose's, look dreadfully dull."

Rommy didn't join in the laughter. "But presents aren't the same as being here. Primrose is right about that. I'd rather have Papa leading an ordinary, boring life and see him more than twice a year. A pearl locket is all well and good, but if anything happens, I have to handle it—alone. I'd think I'd rather have a father who was here even if he was a little less dashing."

Francie put her arm around Rommy's shoulders. "I know you do, but your father loves you. He would be here if he could, which is why we are going to get you to your father's offices."

Rommy stood. "We'd better come up with a good plan because if I know Primrose, she'll be looking for an opportunity to get us in trouble."

Still on the bed, Francie got to her knees and grabbed Rommy's hands. "I think we can cover it up, and nobody will even know you've been gone. You should go tomorrow. It's Saturday and it will be less noticeable if you don't have classes."

"But I have fencing practice tomorrow afternoon," said Rommy.

"I'll tell Monsieur Bouvier you have female complaints. He'll be so embarrassed, he won't ask another thing!"

"Francie, I can't believe you would have the guts to actually say that. Won't you be completely mortified?"

"It's the best way to get a male to stop asking questions." Francie grinned and scrambled off the bed to get her school notebook.

"Even if we fool Monsieur Bouvier, how do I leave Chattingham's unnoticed? And how will I get from Tottenham all the way to Victoria Docks? Papa's offices are on King Street which is almost right on the docks."

"They opened a rail line to the Port of London a while ago," said Francie. "It shouldn't be all that difficult to mingle with the people in third class headed to work, especially dressed as a boy. You'll just look like one of the unwashed masses."

Rommy bit her lip. "What if I get caught and kicked out?"

"You won't," said Francie, jotting down notes. "You just leave the planning to me. We'll get you to those offices, and nobody will be the wiser."

Rommy grabbed Francie's hand, stilling her pen. "Thanks you. I know you're taking a big chance too. If you get caught, you'll get into trouble at school and at home."

Francie gave Rommy's hand a quick squeeze and then pulled it away to continue writing. "We need to get you into the back of the milk wagon when it comes to do the morning delivery. That will get you out of Chattingham's with no one seeing you."

Francie jotted down notes and Rommy leaned in. "I hope you never go over to a life of crime, Francie. You're rather terrifying."

Francie just grinned.

8

THE CLOSE CALL

Rommy opened her eyes to find Francie with a candle in her hand, staring at her. "What time is it?" Rommy murmured.

"It's just after 3 a.m. Everyone is asleep," said Francie. "I checked."

Rommy sat up and rubbed her eyes. "Do you really think I need to go hide now? I thought you said Mrs. Stackhouse said the milkman doesn't make his delivery until 5 a.m."

"You need to be in place, in case he gets here early. You don't want to cut it too close."

Rommy climbed out of bed and splashed water on her face. "I hope I don't fall asleep waiting."

"You won't. I'm coming with you to make sure everything goes according to plan." Francie gave Rommy a knowing smile. "And to make sure you don't chicken out and change your mind."

Rommy donned her fencing clothes and sat down so Francie could fix her hair. Francie had lit a few more candles. The school strictly regulated gas and would notice any extra use.

"We need to make sure your hair stays up nice and tight," Francie said as she ran a brush through Rommy's tangled hair. "You're going to need to keep that cap on so nobody realizes you're a girl. If your hair comes down, the jig is up. People will ask too many questions."

Rommy glanced at the cap lying on her room-mate's bed as Francie braided her hair. "Where did you get a boy's hat?"

"Billy was only too happy to loan it to me," Francie said, smirking.

"Billy, the stable boy?" Rommy asked. "Do I even want to know how you got him to give you his hat?"

Francie giggled. "You'd be surprised at how much boys like flattery and admiration."

Rommy's eyes watered as Francie continued braiding her hair. When she got to the end, Rommy felt a lot of tugging and pulling.

When Rommy looked into the mirror, her hair looked as short as a boy's. It was tightly braided to her head, and Francie had woven the ends up through the original braid. Francie jabbed in several large hair pins at various angles. Then she stood back to look at her creation.

"There," she said. "I think that will stay."

"I hope so," said Rommy. "I can barely blink as it is."

"Stop complaining," said Francie. "Let's make sure you have what you need."

The girls opened Rommy's satchel and Francie went through the items one by one: a flask of water, bread and cheese she had kept back from afternoon tea, 15 shillings, a compass, and two roughly drawn maps, one of the railway stops and one from the last stop to Victoria Dock. Rommy picked up the cap off the bed and added it to the bag.

Francie pulled out the maps and opened them up again near the candle. "Make sure you don't get off too early or you'll end up on Hazel Avenue. That's a long walk to Victoria Dock. You want to ride the railway to the very last stop."

"Do you think anyone will ask questions? Maybe it would be better if I didn't ride the railway the whole way."

"You can't do that, Rommy," said Francie. "Canning Town is near the docks. The closer you get, the dodgier things get. Pickpockets will be the least of your worries, especially if anyone spies that you're a girl, not a boy. Trust me, you don't want to be wandering around those streets by yourself. Not to mention, it's very easy to get lost—lots of dead ends and alleys leading who knows where."

"Won't I have to walk once I get off the train?

Papa's offices aren't on the docks. They're on King Street."

"It will only be a short walk. Remember, Victoria Dock Street to Queen Street to King Street. It's only a block from your stop." Francie had flipped the paper over and was roughly drawing the streets with arrows to show Rommy which way to go. Rommy stared at her.

"How does the daughter of a clergyman know how to make her way around the docks?"

Francie grinned. "It pays to have older brothers - adventurous older brothers - even if they usually are a pain in my bum."

Taking a last look around, Francie grabbed Rommy's dressing gown. "Here, put this over your clothes. If someone happens to be up wandering around, you don't want to look like you are off to fight in a fencing match."

Rommy slipped the gown over her clothes. "Won't they notice I have boots on, and I'm rather lumpy?"

Francie shrugged. "It's still dark. Hopefully, they won't look too closely."

Rommy blew out the candles, plunging the room into shadowy darkness. Francie opened the door. Quietly, the two crept out into the hallway and paused to listen. All was quiet. The grandfather clock's ticking echoed in the silence.

They tiptoed along the hallway, carefully

avoiding the squeaky boards near their friend Eleanore's room. Silently, they crept down the stairs. On the second landing, Rommy grabbed Francie's sleeve. "Did you hear something?" she whispered.

The two paused, straining their ears. A faint creak came from the floor above their heads. Rommy felt a bubble of panic in her chest.

Francie put her finger on her lips and tipped her head, listening. All was quiet again. "It must have been the house settling," she said.

The two continued down until they reached the main floor.

Francie put her hand on Rommy's arm and the two paused again, listening. Everything was silent. Rommy pulled at the neck of her dressing gown. Between it and her fencing outfit, she was hot and itchy. She'd be glad to get rid of one layer, at least.

They had just crossed into the entryway of the school when a whisper of fabric caught Rommy's attention. She whirled around to find Primrose looming behind them. Frantically, she slipped the satchel behind her back. Francie stepped in front of her, helping to hide the bulky bag.

"I knew you two were up to something, so I decided to stay up to keep watch," Primrose said, a malicious gleam in her eye. "And I was right."

Rommy took a sliding step backward and then another.

"I don't know what you're talking about, Primrose," said Francie, a trifle too loudly. "Rommy isn't feeling well. We were headed to the kitchen for a cup of tea."

Rommy dropped the bag onto the floor using her foot to slow its descent while Francie was talking. She hoped Francie's voice covered any sound. A pair of potted palms stood against the wall, and Rommy used her foot to push the bag behind the planters. If Primrose looked closely she'd be able to see it, but Rommy hoped the shadows in the dark hall helped hide the satchel.

"She doesn't look sick to me," said Primrose, squinting at Rommy. "And why is your hair like that?"

Rommy groaned and leaned against the wall.

"Braiding your hair makes the best curls," said Francie. She put a solicitous arm around Rommy's shoulders. "Come on, Rommy. Let's get you that tea."

Francie led Rommy down the hallway toward the dining room. Primrose followed close on their heels. "I don't know what you are up to," said Primrose, "but you won't get away with it."

The three girls turned the corner into the dining room. They all froze.

A light was bobbing across the darkness toward them.

9
THE ESCAPE

Rommy looked wildly at Francie. There was no place to go unless they turned and ran back the way they'd come, and then there was Primrose.

Francie's eyes met Rommy's. With Primrose's attention on the bobbing light, Francie took the opportunity to lean in close to Rommy's ear. "Just follow my lead and try to look sick."

Rommy didn't have time to ask any more questions because the small, round figure of Mrs. Stackhouse materialized out of the gloom of the dining room.

Spotting the three girls, Mrs. Stackhouse gave a start. "Oh my goodness!" she exclaimed. "What are the three of you doing wandering around in the middle of the night?" She held up her candle and peered at them.

Rommy tried to look ill. She felt perspiration

gathering on her forehead. She wasn't sure if it was from nerves or the layers of clothes she was wearing.

Primrose pushed forward. "I saw these two sneaking out of their room, so I followed them. I know they're up to no good. I saw them plotting something at lunch. They even had a map." She shot a triumphant look at Francie.

"I'm not sure what Primrose is talking about. Maybe she was having a bad dream. You really shouldn't have eaten so much pudding at tea." Francie directed a sweet smile at Primrose. "Rommy wasn't feeling very well, so we came down to get a cup of tea. I thought that might help." Her arm was still around Rommy's shoulders.

Mrs. Stackhouse held the candle up higher and peered at Rommy's face. "Sure and you look flushed, dear." She clucked her tongue sympathetically. "Maybe I should fetch the nurse to have a look at you."

"Oh no, Mrs. Stackhouse," said Francie.

"Yes, that's a good idea," said Primrose at the same time.

Mrs. Stackhouse raised an eyebrow.

Francie, catching herself, dropped her voice and her eyes. "I don't think it is anything too serious." She leaned closer. "You know how it is with... female problems..."

Rommy felt her face turning redder, and she

didn't have to pretend to be mortified. Behind her, she heard Primrose snort.

Mrs. Stackhouse gave a chuckle. "Oh yes, dear, I completely understand. I'll just come back to make that tea for you, and I'll get you a bit of birch bark tincture." She paused and looked at Primrose. "I'm not sure what you're about, young miss, but I can handle these two from here with no help from you."

"But Mrs. Stackhouse..." sputtered Primrose.

"I'll thank you to return to your room without delay," she said. "You're lucky I don't report you to Mrs. Wilkes." She held up a hand to ward off Primrose's protest. "Sure and you were trying to be helpful, no doubt, but off with you now."

Without waiting for an answer, she turned around and headed back toward the kitchen.

Rommy and Francie exchanged a look. Primrose glared at them. "You won't get away with this," she said. With a huff, she turned on her heel and headed back toward the main staircase.

Rommy felt panic clawing at her throat and was sure her anxiety must show on her face. What if Primrose looked behind the potted plant and found her satchel? And how would she ever climb into the milk wagon with Mrs. Stackhouse sitting right there?

Francie just shook her head and motioned for Rommy to follow the cook's retreating figure.

Once in the kitchen, Mrs. Stackhouse pointed to the table where Rommy slid into a chair. "I'll just put the kettle on." She made a shooing gesture at Francie. "Go sit with your friend. She looks ready to topple off her chair."

It was true, but not for the reason Mrs. Stackhouse supposed. Rommy's nerves were screaming for her to run. Instead, she scrunched down in her chair and tucked her booted feet beneath the hem of her dressing gown. Her heart was thumping so loudly it was a wonder it didn't wake the whole school.

She willed Mrs. Stackhouse not to look too closely at her. Surely, the woman would wonder why she was wearing her boots or notice that she was considerably thicker than normal. She hunched down further, trying to keep as much of herself from view as possible.

Francie sat next to her and patted her hand. Rommy met her eyes. Her panic must have been plain to see because Francie mouthed, "Trust me."

"You don't have to stay with us, Mrs. Stackhouse," Francie said. "I don't want to keep you up. You looked like you were headed to bed. Were you working extra late?"

"Tish tosh," Mrs. Stackhouse said waving her hand at Francie. "It won't hurt me to stay up a few more minutes. And lands no, I wasn't working until the wee hours. I woke up and remembered that the milkman was coming this morning, and I hadn't unlocked the storage bin for the bottles. He couldn't very well just leave them on the back porch."

The kettle whistled and Mrs. Stackhouse whisked it off the burner. Rummaging in the cupboard, she pulled out two cups and measured out the tea and put it to steep in the kettle.

She settled her bulk on the chair across from Rommy. "Do you always have a hard time with your monthly?" she asked kindly.

Rommy's cheeks burned and she wanted to hit Francie. "Um, well..."

Mrs. Stackhouse smiled at her. "Oh, no need to be embarrassed, dear. Lots of girls have a difficult time of it. Now promise me you won't hesitate to ask Miss Temple for a tincture of birch bark when you're having a hard time of it. You'll find it very helpful as you'll see, and there's no need to be embarrassed. You wouldn't be the first to ask for it."

"Thank you," Rommy mumbled, her eyes firmly fastened to the tabletop.

Mrs. Stackhouse chuckled again as she got up from the chair and strained the tea. Reaching into another cupboard, she pulled down a small box and plucked out a brown vial. She carefully put several drops of the bottle's contents into one cup and set it in front of Rommy. "Drink that up, now," she said. "That should help you feel better."

She set the other cup in front of Francie. "You, too," she said. "Drink up. Tea always helps you sleep."

"Thank you, Mrs. Stackhouse," said Francie. She

took a dainty sip of the tea. Rommy followed her example and almost spit hers out.

"Oh my," said Mrs. Stackhouse seeing Rommy's face. "I forgot the tincture makes it ever so bitter. I'll get you a little honey."

As she got up a loud crash came from the dining room.

"What in the world…" Mrs. Stackhouse said.

The three of them rushed to the kitchen doorway, and looked out into the dining room. At first nothing looked out of place, but then Rommy pointed to a table by the far wall. Several of the chairs lay on their sides.

Before anyone could say anything, the sound of a door slamming echoed from a distant room.

"I think that came from the classroom wing," said Francie.

"It most certainly did. What anyone's doing over there at this time of night, I'd like to know," said Mrs. Stackhouse. Her mouth thinned into a firm line. She turned and pointed a finger at Francie and Rommy. "I want you two to go straight back to your rooms now." Glancing at Rommy, she added in a softer tone, "You can take your tea with you, if you must, but I don't want any dawdling."

Both girls nodded their heads, and Mrs. Stackhouse turned away. "That Primrose up to mischief, no doubt," she muttered as she bustled across the dining room.

As soon as the girls were back in the kitchen, Rommy said, "Who was that, do you think?"

Francie shrugged. "I have no idea, but whoever it was, did us a big favor! We need to hurry and hide."

"Maybe we should scrap this whole thing and try another night. What if Mrs. Stackhouse comes back?"

"Do you really want to do this all over again? Here give me your dressing gown and let's get out of this kitchen before anything else happens."

"We have to go back for my satchel," said Rommy.

Francie shook her head. "We need to wait until we know Mrs. Stackhouse is truly gone. Let's find a place to wait, and then I'll go back and get it."

Francie headed toward the back door. She looked around to find something to slip between it and the jamb so it wouldn't shut and lock behind them. Picking up a small wooden spoon, she slipped it in the door frame as she pulled the door almost shut.

"How are you going to get back to our room?" Rommy asked. "Do you think Primrose will wait for you and raise the alarm?"

"Leave that to me," said Francie. "The important thing is to get you into that milk wagon, and we need to get hidden before he gets here. I have no idea what time it is."

"The milkman must leave the delivery here," said Rommy, pointing at a large metal storage box. "Where's a good place to hide?"

The two girls looked around. A small storage closet at the end of the covered porch caught Rommy's eye. "Maybe this will work." She pulled on the door handle, half expecting it to be locked, but it swung open with a squeak.

They both crowded inside. Odds and ends filled the space. Rommy found a bucket, upturned it and sat down. Francie found a matching one but instead of joining her, she pointed at Rommy.

"You wait," Francie said. "I'll get that satchel before it's too late."

Rommy watched Francie slip out the door and heard the creak of the kitchen door opening. It seemed like forever before Francie poked her head back around the shed door.

"Here it is," she said, holding the bag in front of her like a prize.

"Did you have any trouble?" asked Rommy. "Was Primrose lurking anywhere?"

"Thankfully, no," said Francie. "If that was her making all that racket, she actually helped us. I'm sure that would shrivel her liver if she knew, though."

"Whoever did it, I'm thankful, even if it was Primrose," Rommy said.

The two lapsed into silence. Rommy's eyes felt heavy. A clattering sound outside jerked her back into full alertness. The milkman had arrived.

Francie got up and put her eye to the door. "He's here," she hissed. "Get ready."

They could hear the milk jugs clinking together as the milkman moved them from his wagon to the metal storage box. He made several trips.

"I had no idea we drank that much milk," Francie said.

There was a muffled thump as the man shut the back gate of his wagon.

"Come on," Francie said.

She carefully opened the door and the two slipped out, trying not to let the door squeak on its hinges. This was the trickiest part. If the milkman turned, he'd see them.

"Do you have everything?" Francie mouthed the words.

Rommy nodded her head, then paused and impulsively hugged Francie.

Francie hugged her back and then pushed her toward the back of the wagon, cupping her hands.

Francie gave a grunt as she boosted Rommy up and Rommy flung her leg over the gate. She hadn't even pulled her other leg in when the wagon started to move. Once inside, Rommy sat down and waved at Francie who waved back.

The wagon picked up speed and clattered with its passenger down the lane, out the front gate, and away from Chattingham's.

10
THE BOY

Rommy felt like she might turn into butter with all the bouncing and bumping as the wagon made brisk time into the heart of Tottenham.

Peeking over the gate, she looked around. Despite knowing she should keep hidden, it was hard not to want a better look at the bustling little town. Even this early on a Saturday, the outlying streets showed signs of life. A young boy was shouting from the corner, hawking his papers to passersby.

As they headed toward the center of the small town, they passed a small market where fruits, vegetables, eggs and fresh butter were for sale. Rommy wished she had time to get out and explore, but knew she couldn't miss her train.

Rommy felt herself tensing as the streets got busier. She could tell they were getting closer to the town square. She ducked down again. It wouldn't do for someone to see her.

As they turned a corner, a basket of empty bottles ran into her shin, and she yelped. Straightening, she looked out the back gate again. A tall boy with dark, shaggy hair caught her eye. He looked to be a year or two older than she was, but that wasn't what had caught her attention. He seemed to be looking right at her.

Rommy slid down until she was almost lying flat. She clutched her satchel to her chest. Her heart felt like it had tripled its beat. She twisted to get a little more comfortable and her locket slid sideways.

Reaching into the neck of her shirt, she pulled it out and gripped it tightly. The little pearl dug into her palm.

Rommy took a deep breath and then another. Her heart slowed. How silly she was being. Even if some random boy saw her, what was he going to do? From what she remembered from her quick glimpse, he looked kind of shabby. It's not like he'd go running to a constable.

Cautiously, she scooted back to a sitting position and peered out. Just as she thought, the boy was nowhere to be found.

As they turned a corner, Lucille's Tea Room came into view. Rommy gave a start as she realized this was her stop, so to speak. Francie had said she should look for Lucille's, and if she went past the apothecary, she had gone too far.

Pulling her satchel over her shoulder, Rommy wanted to smack herself. She should have been considering how she would get out of a moving wagon before the time actually came to do it.

She didn't want to hit the ground and go rolling. Surely, that would attract too much attention - even if people thought she was a boy.

Rommy crouched. She could probably climb over the gate and then jump. Hopefully, she'd land on her feet.

Should she wait for a busy section or a less crowded area? What would draw the least attention?

As she was deciding, the wagon lurched to a stop and she heard the driver yelling, "Whoa, there, Bess! What are you doing, lad? Are you trying to meet your maker?"

Rommy fell against the wooden gate. She couldn't see who the milkman was shouting at, but whoever it was solved her problem.

Righting herself, she scrambled out of the wagon and hopped down, hurrying onto the sidewalk. Looking back and forth, she spotted the entrance to the Underground in the town's center.

Mindful of the milkman's tirade, she looked both ways before crossing the street, careful to watch where she stepped. Reaching the Underground's entrance, she flew down the steps and then stopped at the bottom and dug out her cap. Jamming it on her head, she walked into the tube station.

A cavernous area opened up. On one end was a line of ticket windows and on the other a platform hugged the tracks. Crowds of people bustled between the two. Dodging between bodies, she hurried over to one of the windows on the end that wasn't busy. A bored man looked down at her.

"I'd like a ticket to Victoria Docks, please," she said.

"Looking for work, are you?" the clerk asked, reaching to get her ticket. "You speak well enough, but I doubt they'll have use for a lad your size."

Rommy wasn't sure what to say. Of course, the clerk thought she was heading to the docks to find a job. She knew she didn't sound like a boy looking for work, but it was too late for that now.

"Yes, sir," she said. "I may be small, but I work hard. I'm quick, too."

The clerk chuckled and handed her the ticket. "Well, good luck to you, then. Remember, though, the last line comes back to Tottenham at 7 p.m. You'd best be on it unless you want to spend the night in Canning Town. Nobody wants to do that."

Rommy thanked him, took the ticket and headed toward the benches on the platform. Her stomach rumbled. She hadn't eaten breakfast. It had been so early and she'd been so nervous, eating hadn't even crossed her mind. Thankfully, Francie had thought of food.

Thinking of her friend, Rommy worried she might get caught. She hoped Francie could keep her absence a secret. What if Primrose had been waiting for them and realized Rommy was gone? What would she do if she got caught and Mrs. Wilkes kicked her out?

Rommy pulled an apple out of her bag and munched on it, her mind back at Chattingham's. She wished there was some way to get in touch with Francie. The large clock over the ticket booths said it was almost 7 a.m. Everyone would still be asleep on a Saturday. Breakfast wasn't until 8:30 on the weekends.

Well, there was nothing she could do about it now, Rommy thought. She just needed to get to the docks and find out what had happened to her father, or at least where he was at. She had to be back at the Underground by 7 p.m. That was a whole twelve hours from now.

Rommy bit into the last of the apple and got up to find a trash barrel. As she turned from the bench, she spotted the tall boy. He seemed to be looking at her again.

Did he see through her disguise? Act like nothing is wrong, she told herself, as she walked from the trash barrel to another bench. By now, crowds of men and boys bunched into groups along the platform.

The train let out a loud whistle that made her jump. Worming her way into the crowd waiting to board the train, she jostled through the throng of bodies into the railcar with the rest.

Surrounded by so many people taller than she was, she couldn't see if the boy was around or not. At first, Rommy felt like she was fighting against a strong tide with the crush of bodies scrambled for seats on the benches.

She eventually made her way toward the back of the crowded car and found an unoccupied corner. Perched there, she hugged her satchel to her chest. The train lurched forward with a belch of smoke, and she hung onto the back of the bench.

Rommy chided herself for being paranoid. It wasn't unusual for someone to take this line toward Central London or the docks to find work. Of course, that was what that boy was doing. It had nothing to do with her.

Despite her reassurances to herself, though, she couldn't get over the itchy feeling he was watching her.

As the train chugged along, Rommy felt her eyes getting heavy. She had been up since the wee hours, and the motion of the train lulled her into a light doze.

Rommy's head jerked up with a start when the train came to an abrupt stop and the conductor bellowed out the Hazel Avenue stop. She dug out the map Francie had given her. There was only one more stop before she had to get off. She tucked the map back into her bag.

Rommy turned her body as far to the side as she could when a group of men pushed past her to exit the train. They streamed out the door and the car emptied until only about half the passengers were left.

It was then she spotted him. He was sitting on the far side of the car. His dark eyes were fixed on her face.

Rommy's heart picked up speed again. He smiled slowly and winked at her.

Without another thought, Rommy lurched to her feet and slid out the train doors just as they closed. She didn't know who that boy was, but her gut, the same gut that told her when an opponent was about to strike, told her he was trouble. The more space she put between them, the better.

II
THE BULLY

Rommy ran up the steps of the railway station. The sound hit her first. It rushed over her like a wave. There was the clatter of wagons, the ringing of the trolley's bell, and the hustle and bustle of what appeared to be the whole world going about its business. It was so loud, for a moment, Rommy felt dazed.

The next thing that hit her was the smell. The good and the bad mixed in an intoxicating blend that couldn't decide whether to be pleasant or disgusting. She stood trying to get her bearings.

This had not been part of the plan. She clutched her satchel against her side and dug out the map Francie had shoved into her hand before she had left.

Francie and Chattingham's seemed very far away at the moment, and Rommy felt small and alone. She could get swallowed up in London and nobody would ever know where she was and what happened. Fear crawled up her spine and lodged right behind her breast bone.

She froze for a moment, and then, out of the corner of her eye, she saw a familiar shadow.

That boy again.

Was he following her?

It was too much of a coincidence that he would be in Tottenham, then on the railway, and now getting off at the same stop.

Several boys near her age streamed by her. She shook her head. He was probably just one more person looking for work in the city.

Tottenham had put in the line to Central London and the docks for just that reason - to get workers into the city.

Rommy squared her shoulders. According to the map, she needed to head south toward the Thames River. The docks and all the offices and warehouses were close by. She had gotten off only one stop too early.

Even if she got lost, the Thames was rather hard to miss, so she'd just keep going until she found it. She headed down the walkway, careful to stay away from the curb. The wagons and buggies created a constant stream of traffic. That didn't include the public transportation.

Rommy stopped and stared as a double-decker

bus went by pulled by four horses. A man brushed by her, almost knocking her off her feet. "Quit gawping, lad," the man scolded as he hurried on.

Rommy picked up her pace. She wasn't sure how far it was to the Victoria Docks, but the sooner she got there, the sooner she could get back to Chattingham's before someone discovered she was gone.

The further she walked, the shabbier the storefronts got. After what seemed like a dozen blocks, the people started to look shabbier too. Men and women stood on the street corners hawking different wares.

Rommy put her head down and hurried past as they called to her and other passersby. A store front window caught her eye. In the reflection she saw the same boy who had been on the train. Her heart thudded. This couldn't be a coincidence.

He was following her.

She ducked into an alley and hurried deeper into the maze of back streets. If she cut across, maybe she could lose him and then return to her original route.

Unfortunately, the alleys were a maze with no straight paths. Rommy made a right turn, but found herself facing, not the street, but a dead end. Backtracking, she turned down another alley that emptied into a narrow lane with tenements lining each side. Her eyes burned from the smell. A young woman looked toward her, shook her head and then emptied a bucket of something foul into the street where it ran into a center indent. Ragged children ran barefoot through greasy puddles. She ducked back into the alley, intent on getting back to the main street.

Rommy berated herself. She should have gone into one of the stores, not an alley. She had no idea where she was and was now hopelessly turned around. She wanted to sit down and cry, but she couldn't. Who knew what would happen if anyone realized she didn't belong here, or that she was a girl from a fancy boarding school.

Rommy looked up at the sky, hoping to get an idea from the position of the sun, but the alleys and streets were so narrow, the sky was only a thin sliver overhead. A permanent twilight lingered in these back pathways.

"I ain't giving it to you! I earned it fair and square," a young voice yelled.

Ugly laughter answered, followed by a shrill scream.

Rommy hesitated only a moment before running toward the sound.

In a dead end alley, a small girl was surrounded by a ring of boys. They reminded Rommy of the pack of feral dogs that sometimes hung around the school's compost heap. The girl who looked to be maybe five years old, if that, was sitting on the ground holding the side of her face.

Despite being outnumbered and outsized, she was glaring ferociously up at the leader of the group, a thick boy with a thatch of straw-colored hair.

"Give me my bread back," she demanded. "The lady gave it to me!"

"Shut up! It's our bread now." The boy towered over her menacingly.

Instead of cowering, the girl hopped to her feet, and lunged at the bread.

One of the other boys grabbed her by the back of her thin dress and hoisted her off her feet. Her feet kicked out, catching the leader in the stomach.

He growled in her face. "You'll pay for that, you little runt."

Turning to the other boy, he ordered, "Hold her while I teach her a little lesson."

He smiled as another boy grabbed onto the little girl, immobilizing her as the big boy advanced, his fist balled up.

Before she could think what she was doing, Rommy grabbed up a long piece of wood that had fallen off a boarded up window. Charging forward, she used the board to smack the boy nearest her that was holding onto the girl.

He yelped and let go of the little girl's arm. Off balance, the other boy dropped her onto the ground. The girl scrambled to her feet, took in the situation and ran to stand behind Rommy.

The five boys stared at Rommy for a moment. Rommy felt very small, looking up at them. They were all at least a head taller than she was.

The leader, recovering from his surprise, sneered. "What do we have here? A hero to the rescue, eh?"

Rommy lifted her chin. "It takes a lot of courage for five big boys to beat up on a little girl. You should be so proud of yourselves."

"Shut your pie hole," said the leader. "This ain't none of your business. It looks like you need a lesson, too. Little toffs like you don't belong here." He cracked his knuckles and advanced.

"I give you fair warning," said Rommy. "I don't want to hurt you. The little girl and I will just be leaving."

"You ain't going anywhere," he snarled, "and we ain't the ones that's going to be hurting."

As the group advanced toward her, Rommy leaped onto an overturned crate. The little girl needed no urging and scrambled behind the stack of crates.

The board was heavier than her fencing blade, so her timing was off. But she smacked the arm of the leader hard enough to make him howl as he made a grab for her. He lost his balance, and the little girl, darting out from behind the crates, stuck out her foot. He went down with a thud. Dancing to the left, Rommy knocked another boy in the back of the head and he went down too.

She wasn't used to having to hit quite so hard or do more than getting a touch in. This was much heavier work than fencing.

Rommy knew she had to stay on her feet if she had any chance of coming out of this encounter with nothing broken or permanently damaged.

Two of the five boys were rolling on the cobble stones of the alley, including the leader. But three still stood, although the smallest one looked ready to bolt given the chance. All three were giving her some distance, eyeing her and her makeshift sword.

Rommy saw what they were planning before they did it. Maybe it was the way they looked at each other or a subtle nod of heads, but she knew the two on the ends were going to rush her.

She waited until they were so close their fingers were brushing her shirt. Then she leaped back and whirled, hitting one in the back with the board and knocking him into his partner. The two hit the ground in a tangle of legs and arms.

Unfortunately, in the excitement, she forgot to keep her eye on the two on the ground. One moment she was savoring the thrill of victory, and the next she was flat on her back. Her head thumped painfully against the ground and her hat popped off her head. She felt a flutter of panic. Without her hat, was it obvious she was a girl?

The leader, quick to use his advantage, was strad-dling her chest before she could scramble to her feet.

He sneered at her. "Not so tough now, are you, pretty boy?"

Rommy still had hold of her board, but the bully's

knees were pinning her arms. She was also finding it difficult to breath with all of his weight pinning her down. Behind him she could see the other three getting to their feet.

The metallic taste of fear flooded her mouth as the boy's face and fist filled her vision. This wouldn't be good. What would they do to her? Would they kill her or just beat her senseless? How would she ever get back to Chattingham's if they broke her arm or her leg or....at this point her imagination failed her. She squeezed her eyes shut.

12
THE RESCUE

Suddenly, the weight on Rommy's body disappeared. The boy flew through the air. He hit the wall with a thump and slid motionless to the ground. She laid still, trying to get her breath back. After a moment, she shook her head to clear it. A small hand pulled on her. "Come on! Are you stupid? Get up! Get up!"

Rommy got painfully to her feet and tried to dust the grime off her trousers. Her cap had fallen off, so she grabbed it and jammed it back on her head. Tendrils of hair had come loose and were sticking to her face and neck, but her braid was still intact. Looking around, she recognized the tall boy with shaggy, dark hair standing on top of the pile of crates. A small, fast moving ball of light was making figure eights around him. Rommy squinted. What was that light? Her head was still ringing from the thump it had taken.

Four of the boys were lying in a heap, and the fifth was running away as fast as his legs could carry him.

The little girl was yanking harder on Rommy's hand now. "Come on! Do you have dirt between your ears? We hafta get away from here!"

Rommy stood rooted to the spot, staring at the tall boy. He gave her a jaunty smile and salute. Her paralysis melted into anger.

All the fear of the last few minutes merged with that anger. This boy was to blame for all of this. None of this would have happened if he hadn't been following her.

Carried on that wave of anger, Rommy marched up to him. "Who are you and why are you following me?"

The boy seemed to float down from the crates. "Maybe we should have this chat somewhere else?" He nodded toward the boys stirring a few feet away. A few moans drifted toward them. Rommy crossed her arms and stared at him.

Instead of answering her, he grabbed Rommy's elbow and towed her out of the alley. "Nice work with that board, by the way. If there had been one or two fewer, you might have even won."

Rommy yanked her elbow away and planted her feet. A small body ran into her legs. She looked down into a pair of big blue eyes fringed with long, dark lashes. "We need to get..." she gestured at the small girl, "home to her parents."

"I'm Alice."

"I need to get Alice home to her parents." Rommy looked down at the little girl. "I'm sure they're worried about you."

Alice raised her eyebrows and shook her head. "You may be brave, but you really are thick. I ain't got no parents. What do you think I was doing in that alley? Just chumming around with Danny and his gang for fun?"

"You can't be over five. Surely, you have someone looking after you."

"I'm six and a half, not five!" Alice crossed her arms and rolled her eyes. "And I look after myself which is more than I can say for you." The girl pushed Rommy away from the alleyway from which they had just emerged. Rommy could hear the sounds of movement and voices. They needed to put some distance between themselves and those boys.

Rommy allowed Alice to steer her down another alleyway and up a narrow street. The boy fell into step with her. He had a smirk on his face, clearly amused.

Rommy's anger smoldered into life again. "You still haven't answered my question! Who are you and why are you following me?"

"That's two questions. You can call me Finn when you thank me for saving your life."

"Yes, well, thank you, Finn… wait, how did you know I was a girl?" Ice crept up Rommy's spine.

"It's obvious from the way you…" He gestured toward her lower half.

Rommy looked down at her trousers, confused.

"It's the way you waggle yer bum around when you're walking," said Alice. "You don't walk like a boy at all. They walk more like this." Alice demonstrated by lengthening her stride and slouching with each step. "And you never scratch at yourself neither."

Rommy's face warmed and she cleared her throat. "I guess I must practice, then."

She looked at Alice and then Finn. She couldn't just leave the little girl to wander around these filthy alleyways. What if that gang of boys came back to finish what they started? But how would she sneak back into Chattingham's with a small girl in tow?

She pushed the worry away. The real question was who was Finn and what did he want? It didn't escape her notice that while he had told her his name, he hadn't explained who he was and why he was following her. True, he had saved her and Alice back there, but what did he want?

Rommy reached for her pocket watch and then stopped. She groaned in frustration.

"What's wrong?" asked Finn.

"My satchel," said Rommy. "I must have dropped it back in the alleyway. It has all my belongings and my map! I have to go back for it." She spun on her heel, but Finn gripped her arm.

"You may as well say goodbye to whatever you had in there," said Finn. "Danny and his gang will have taken it and be long gone by now."

Rommy tried to pull her arm way, but his grip was too tight. She grabbed one of his fingers and yanked it backward.

"Ow!" He pulled his hand away, shaking it. The small ball of light that had been buzzing around him, zoomed at Rommy making a loud, chittering sound. Startled, she covered her head with her hands. Finn made a series of clicks and whistles, and the small light returned to hover near his shoulder. It was still chittering loudly.

"What is that thing?" asked Rommy.

"Do you have a pet firefly or something?" asked Alice. She clapped her hands in delight at the idea.

Finn whistled again and the small ball of light zipped off. "It's a she, not a thing," he said.

"Well, what is *she*?" asked Rommy.

"A fairy," Finn answered.

13
THE DESTINATION

Rommy laughed. She couldn't help it. "A fairy? You really expect me to believe that?"

The little ball of light dimmed. An angry look flashed across Finn's face. "Don't say that! Belief keeps them alive!" He cupped his hand protectively over the small light that had perched on his shoulder.

"Ooh," said Alice, fascinated, "can I see her?" She stood on her tiptoes to peer at the being on Finn's shoulder.

Finn made another series of clicks and squeals, and then he squatted down next to Alice.

She leaned in, her blue eyes large and solemn. "Hello," she said. "I'm Alice."

Tinkling sounds spilled into the air, and the light drew closer to Alice.

Rommy couldn't help it. She took a step closer. Of

course she didn't believe this, whatever it was, could possibly be a fairy, but she was curious.

Casually, she leaned forward, and then, startled, drew back as the ball of light flew straight at her face, only swerving at the last moment. In the blur of movement, Rommy caught the outline of a tiny girl and wings. She blinked in surprise.

"Ouch!" she yelped as pain shot from her scalp. The small ball of light clicked and whistled, sounding somehow angry.

Several of Rommy's tawny hairs hung from the zipping light.

"I guess Nissa doesn't like what you said," said Finn. He crossed his arms and cocked an eyebrow. He didn't even have to say I told you so.

"Fairy or no fairy, I need to go to the docks," said Rommy. She turned in a circle. They were standing in a narrow back street. Unlike the street that had been teeming with small children and their mothers, this one was eerily silent and lined with darkened doorways. More alleyways and crooked streets branched out around her, but by this time, she was completely lost. She had no idea which way would lead back to the main road or even which way to go once she reached it.

"Whatcha want with the docks?" asked Alice. She was still staring at Nissa, and she kept making cooing sounds trying to get the fairy to come closer.

"My father's offices are over there." Rommy

thought the less detail she gave the better. She still didn't know who Finn was and what he wanted. The fairy didn't lessen her suspicions about him.

"Your father won't be there," said Finn.

"How would you know anything about my father?"

"I know more than you do," he said with one of his maddening smiles. "And he's not there."

Rommy's stomach sank. "I know he likely isn't in his offices, but I'm hoping... that is to say... I was hoping I could find out more information about where he is and when he will be back."

"You won't find out what he's been up to at those dock offices." Again, Finn sounded very sure of himself.

"How do you even know my father? I've never heard him mention your name." Rommy tried to push down the panic rising in her chest. She didn't know where she was, and there was something off about this boy.

"Your father and I go way back," said Finn. He examined his nails. "But not from London."

"Could you please stop speaking in riddles and tell me what you mean? I need to get to the docks and then back to the tube station before the last train leaves for To... I mean for my school."

"You may as well give up that idea," said Finn.

"Which idea? Going to the docks or getting back

to school on time?" Rommy felt like stamping her foot in frustration.

A small hand pulled on her shirt which had come untucked. "Enough jawing. This is the way you need." Alice grabbed Rommy's hand and tried to pull her down one of the alleys that seemed to twist into nowhere. When Rommy refused to move, Alice let out a loud sigh. "Do you want to go to the docks or don'tcha?"

Rommy hesitated, but decided she had no choice but to trust the little girl. She certainly had no idea where she was and the silent street gave her the creeps. Even though she saw no one, it still felt like eyes were watching them.

With a last withering glare at Finn, she let the girl pull her away. "Lead on, Alice. At least you know what's what."

Despite Alice's tiny size, Rommy had to trot to keep up with her as she zipped up one alley and down another, making a series of turns.

Rommy was just worrying that maybe Alice didn't know where she was going when they came out onto the sidewalk. They were not even a block from the alley she had originally ducked into to get away from Finn.

"Oh, thank goodness," she breathed.

"Wotcha - didn't you think I knew where I was going?" Alice seemed put out by this idea.

"Oh no, it's not that. I just hated feeling so lost," Rommy admitted.

"You don't have to worry. I'm better than a map," said Alice. "The docks are this way. Which ones do you need to get to again?"

"The Victoria Docks," Rommy said. "We need to hurry though. I have to get back to the Tube Station before seven, or I'll miss the last train back to school."

The little girl cocked her head. "That's not too far from here," she said. She pointed back over her shoulder toward the twisting maze of alleys they had just left. "We'd git there faster if we was to go through the back way, but we might run into Danny and his gang." Alice put her chin up but not before Rommy saw a slight shiver ripple through the small girl's frame. For all her bravado, Alice was just a little girl.

"No, we mustn't risk it," Rommy agreed.

The two set off down the sidewalk. They hadn't gone more than a block when someone shot out of an alley toward them. Rommy instinctively pushed Alice behind her, wondering if Danny and his friends had found them.

She looked up into a pair of laughing grey eyes. "Oh, it's you. Come on Alice, let's get a move on."

Finn fell into step with them. Rommy didn't look at him. "You weren't invited on this trip," she said.

"Don't mind if I do come along. You'll need my help once you finally accept the truth."

Rommy ignored him and just walked faster, causing Alice to trot now. Nissa zipped around Finn's head and played hide and seek in Alice's long curls. The little girl giggled but didn't slow down.

Finn said nothing. He just lengthened his stride and kept up with ease with his much longer legs.

The further they walked, the shabbier their surroundings got, and the more crowded the streets became.

"King Street is just down there." Finn pointed toward the next intersection. Rommy didn't want to admit it, but with the press of people, mostly men and boys, she was grudgingly glad she and Alice weren't on their own.

Rommy stepped away from him. "Thank you, but I knew that."

Finn just grinned.

14

THE BIG QUESTION

The trio turned down King Street. "There," said Rommy, pointing at a building located toward the end of the block. "That's Papa's office."

She picked up her pace until she was almost running. Alice trotted along beside her panting as she tried to keep up.

Rommy skidded to a halt before a squat square building. The brick sides were smudged with soot and the windows were so dirty, you couldn't see inside.

Rommy walked up the steps to the door and paused. She took a deep breath and turned the handle. At first she thought she was out of luck, but then with a groan, it turned.

The inside was dim, and disappointment stabbed through her. Even though her father wasn't here, she had hoped that his shipping clerk would have been there. She looked around.

There was a small entryway separated from the rest of the office by a waist-high half-wall with a swinging door. Along the far wall was a set of cabinets that held maps. Above that was one large map with various pins stuck into it. There were two desks, a big one against the back wall, and a smaller one closer to the entrance. Both had a forlorn, abandoned air about them.

Rommy pushed the swinging door and drifted into the office area. A thick layer of dust covered everything.

She walked toward the map and peered at the various pins. They all clustered in one place, and someone—her father by the looks of the elegant handwriting— had penned the words "entry point" with a question mark after it.

A cold, sinking feeling started in Rommy's stomach. Her shoulders slumped, and a lump in her throat made swallowing difficult. It was obvious her father had not come into these offices in a long time, much longer than since his last visit.

Alice sneezed making Rommy jump. She had almost forgotten about Finn and Alice.

"Are you sure you have the right place?" Alice asked, looking at the trail of wood now visible where she had just wiped her hand. "Ain't nobody been here in ages."

"This is his office," Rommy said. She shook her head. "I don't understand. He was here at Christmas and that was only five months ago. His clerk, Mr. Smee, should have been in here, at least a few days a week."

Finn let out a whoop of laughter. "Mr. Smee? A shipping clerk?" he wheezed out.

"What's so funny?" Her dismay was quickly turning to panic. This had been her one hope of finding her father, and now, it looked as if he hadn't been here in years. She was sick with disappointment. She didn't understand what was going on, but the panicky desperation choking her needed a target. And the boy laughing so hard he could barely stand seemed as good as any.

She stomped over to him and using both hands, shoved him as hard as she could. He fell to the floor with a satisfying thump. Rommy batted away Nissa, who came zooming at her chittering and squealing. "Leave me alone, you little bug!"

She crossed her arms and glared at Finn. "And you—you better tell me what you know."

"I've been trying to tell you, Miss Know-it-all. Your father isn't who you think he is. He isn't in London, and the seas he sails aren't the Atlantic."

"What are you talking about? You're not making any sense. What other waters would he sail? Are you saying he is going to India or the Orient?" Rommy was confused. "Why would he go there? Our properties are in the Caribbean."

"Your father hasn't visited there in over a decade," said Finn. "He's too busy fighting Lost Boys with his band of pirates."

"Pirates?" Rommy's voice climbed to an undignified screech but she couldn't seem to help it. "Are you mad? My father was an admiral in the Queen's Navy in his youth. He would never be a pirate. He caught pirates for goodness' sake!"

"I suppose that explains why he's so good at it," said Finn. "He learned from the best, I suppose. And Mr. Smee? That would be his second in command, not his shipping clerk." A snort escaped Finn before he rearranged his face into a more somber expression.

"My father is not a pirate!" Rommy stamped her foot. "Of all the ridiculous, far-fetched..." she sputtered.

"Ooh, a pirate! How exciting!" said Alice.

Rommy rounded on the little girl. "It's not exciting because he's not a pirate. He's a sea captain, and he's gone because he has to sail to our land in St. Croix." Even to her own ears, her words sounded desperate.

"Don't take a bite out of me," said Alice. "It ain't my fault yer father's told you a whopper."

Rommy felt as if someone had slapped her. "He...

he... he hasn't told a whop... I mean lied to me. There must be an explanation." She put up her hand to stop Finn from speaking. "An explanation that makes sense. Not some fantastical story that he's a pirate."

Finn had gotten up and was leaning against the bank of cabinets. Now he shrugged his shoulders. "Believe it or not, but if you want to see your father, I can take you there."

"If he's some pirate roaming the Seven Seas, how are you going to take me to him?"

Finn's hand moved so fast, Rommy hardly realized what he was doing until he had snagged Nissa in his fist. The fairy didn't sound too happy about it either.

Finn walked toward Rommy. He looked so determined, Rommy wanted to take a step back, but she held her ground.

"Well, you're going to have to trust me and exercise your belief muscles." He reached out and plucked the cap off her head and tossed it onto the nearby desk.

"Belief muscles? What are you talking about?"

He lifted the fairy and shook her gently over Rommy's head. A fine sprinkling of golden dust fell over her head and face and down the front of her stained shirt.

"We can't get to your father unless we fly and flying means pixie dust and a little trust. You probably need extra since you aren't too trusting." He shook the unhappy fairy again. "And close your mouth. Pixie dust doesn't taste very good."

15
THE MAGIC

"Do me next," said Alice, hopping from one foot to another.

Finn looked at her and then at Rommy. "Are we taking her with us?"

"Wait just a minute," Rommy said, brushing at the dust now covering her hair. "I never said I was going with you."

"But I thought you wanted to find your father?" Alice peered at her, puzzled.

Rommy took a deep breath and let it out slowly, trying to rein in her emotions. She'd already snapped at the girl once, and Alice didn't deserve it. None of this was her fault after all.

"I do, but this all seems like a bunch of nonsense." She flung out a hand in Finn's direction. "I've never met this boy in my life. I've never heard my father talk about him or mention anything about him. How dumb would I be to just swallow this entire story?"

Alice raised one eyebrow. "I don't know about dumb, but what else are you going to do?" She gestured around the office. "It don't look like anybody's been here in ages and ages. If you don't go with him, you'll just have to go back to that school of yours. It seems like a lot of trouble for nothing if you ask me."

Rommy turned away from both of them. Her hand closed around her locket, and she rubbed at the pearl absently. Alice was right. What was she supposed to do now? Finn was obviously a raving lunatic, but the idea of going back to school with no answers left her feeling sick.

"If I go, what will happen to Alice?" Rommy asked.

Finn pushed off from the wall and came to stand in front of Rommy. "We can take her with us. I don't see we have much choice. You can't send her back to Danny and his gang."

"I'm right here," said Alice. "You don't have to talk like I'm not here." A bubble of laughter took Rommy by surprise. With her hands on her hips and the sour expression on her face, Alice looked like a miniature Mrs. Wilkes in a scolding mood.

The thought of Mrs. Wilkes drew Rommy up short. Without realizing it, she grabbed onto Finn's arm. "If I go with you, how long will I be gone? I have to get back for the last train. I can't get caught. Francie will never be able to keep my absence a secret for longer than a day, at most."

Finn scratched his head. "I can't promise how long it will take. We are heading for Neverland. Time isn't the same there."

Exasperated, Rommy threw her hands up. "What does that even mean?"

Alice pushed between the two. "Hello - I'm still here."

Finn yelped and opened his hand. "You little blighter. You bit me!"

The fairy let out a series of tinkling chimes. It sounded like she was laughing.

She zipped through the air and circled Alice's head, turning and spinning. A shower of golden dust fell onto Alice's head. The little girl let out a squeal and laughed.

Rommy watched, amazed, as Alice shut her eyes and floated up off the floor. It didn't take long before she was zooming around the offices, tentative at first and then gaining confidence. She did a loop around Rommy's head, laughter trailing after her.

"How.. What.. Are you saying we're *flying* to this Neverland place?"

Finn floated up off the floor toward the ceiling. "Yep. It's the only way to get there. Come on. You can do it too. Just close your eyes and think about flying."

Rommy obediently closed her eyes. The idea was so incredible and so ridiculous, though, she couldn't visualize herself in the air.

Her feet stayed planted on the ground. She opened her eyes. "It doesn't work for me," she said.

Finn alighted next to Rommy. "You have to believe—really believe—you can fly," he said.

"I don't really believe that though," said Rommy.

"Why not? Alice can do it and so can I. Why wouldn't you be able to?"

"Because it's flying. Nobody can fly," said Rommy.

Finn laughed. "But Alice and I are flying right in front of you. So, you're wrong. At least two some-bodies can fly."

Rommy sighed. "I'll try again." She squeezed her eyes shut and muttered under her breath, "I can fly. I can fly. I can fly."

"You're doing it!" said Alice.

Rommy's eyes popped open, and she saw her feet were an inch or two off the floor. "I can't believe it!" Immediately, she thumped back to the ground and stumbled to catch her balance.

Alice landed next to her and stared up at her. "What's wrong with you?"

"I can't do this," said Rommy, putting her hands over her face. "I'll never get to this Neverland place if I can hardly get off the ground."

Finn had floated back up toward the ceiling. He

had crossed his legs, hovering in mid-air, his chin in his hands. He was studying her as if she was something strange from one of her botany classes.

"What?" she asked.

"I think you are too tied to the earth," he said.

"We're all tied to the earth. It's called gravity," she said, rolling her eyes.

"No." Finn shook his head. "You are heavy with the things here. You need to think light thoughts."

"Light thoughts?"

"Like feathers and kites," he said.

"I'll try it, but I doubt it'll work."

Dutifully, she closed her eyes again. She visualized a feather, light as air, floating, floating, floating.

She heard Alice clap her hands and Finn shush her. "That's it," encouraged Finn. "Keep thinking light thoughts."

Rommy thought of her feather riding through the air, carried along by a breeze. She cracked her eyes open and gasped as she realized she was now several feet off the floor. She felt herself faltering.

Finn shouted, "Feathers."

"Light as air," added Alice.

"Kites flying on the wind," said Finn.

Rommy felt herself buoyed back up. She made a tentative swimming action, hesitant at first and then picking up speed.

A delighted laugh burst out. "I can't believe I'm really flying," she said.

As soon as the words, "I can't believe," left her mouth, she felt herself losing altitude again.

"Feathers!" shouted Alice.

"Dandelion fluff," said Finn.

Rommy closed her eyes again and imagined she was dandelion fluff riding the wind. She felt herself rising until the ceiling was brushing the back of her head.

"Just keep thinking light thoughts," said Finn. "Oh, and you need to open your eyes."

Rommy felt her face grow warm. "Of course," she said.

Finn flew toward the back of the offices and opened a window. It protested with a loud squeak and groan. "We'll go out the back way. We'll attract too much attention going out the front door."

Rommy felt a somewhat hysterical giggle rise in her throat. "What makes you say that? I'm sure three children flying out the front door of an abandoned office would be quite normal."

As Finn slipped out the window, Rommy held her hand out to Alice. "Are you coming with us? We should have asked you if you wanted to go."

Alice rolled her eyes. "Of course I am. What would I be doing if I stayed here?" She zipped past Rommy's outstretched hand and out the window. "They have fairies there," she called over her shoulder as she caught up with Finn.

With a last glance at the abandoned office,

Rommy followed. Finn was already high above the building. He and Alice were hovering there, waiting for her, Nissa doing figure eights around the two.

Rommy swallowed her nervousness as a sudden sense of dread filled her. The only life she'd known was about to change, and she didn't know if she wanted it to. Even though she missed Papa all the time, she was used to how things worked at Chattingham's, during her father's visits. What if he wasn't happy to see her? That is, if they even found him.

As she followed Finn and Alice ever higher into the sky above London's bustling streets, Rommy admitted to herself there was no going back to the way things were. Trying to keep her mind off of how very high they were, she let her mind wander to what her father could have been doing all this time. It seemed impossible he was a pirate. Not her noble, gallant Papa. Then again, she was flying, flying of all things, and behind a boy with a fairy. She didn't know what was true anymore.

Rommy put on a burst of speed to catch up to Alice and Finn. One thing she did know. She wasn't coming back without answers.

16
THE ISLAND

It felt like they had been flying forever, yet it seemed she barely had time to blink before Finn began to circle downwards toward a cluster of impossibly pink and purple clouds. Even though they had left London at midday, here it was late afternoon.

Passing through the clouds felt like sliding through a mist. Rommy saw Alice slow down and trail her fingers along the rainbow-washed water suspended in fat droplets all around them.

Then they were through the clouds, and an island spread out before them. Rommy couldn't help gasping.

"Blimey!" said Alice. "What is this place?"

Finn circled back to hover next to them. He folded his arms across his chest and rocked back on his heels. "This is Neverland."

Below them was a turquoise lagoon surrounded by a beach with pink sand. Rocky cliffs rose steadily from the pink beach, and a great round rock sat in the heart of the lagoon.

"We'll land here," said Finn. He headed toward the beach. Rommy and Alice followed more slowly.

Despite her enthusiasm earlier, the little girl grabbed Rommy's hand as they touched down on the sand.

"I've never seen pink sand before," said Rommy.

"I've never seen *any* sand," said Alice. She let go of Rommy's hand and bent over to pick up a handful of the pink grains.

Finn put his finger to his lips and then spoke in a low voice. "Neverland isn't like London," he said. "There is magic, yes, but there are also dangerous things here, too." He nodded his head toward the water. "Like mermaids."

"As if London isn't dangerous," said Alice. "If I can get on the far side of Danny and his gang, yer mermaids don't scare me."

"Keep your voice down," warned Finn. "You don't want them to hear you. They'll lure you into the water if they can."

A wave of water splashed over Rommy's back. The cold made her gasp, and she spun around thinking Alice had done it. Instead, a young woman was treading water in the lagoon. Her black hair rippled around her and she had a smile on her beautiful face. But when Rommy looked into the sea-green eyes, she felt a chill.

"How very disappointing, Finn," she called. "You know we are always so happy to see you. It makes me sad to think you aren't as happy to see us!"

A blonde head popped up next to her. "Finn," she squealed. "Come in and play with us and bring your new friends!"

Finn leaned in closer to the girls. "Don't let them tempt you into the water. They'll drown you."

Rommy looked at the enchanting two creatures now swimming around each other in what looked like a graceful version of tag.

A third head popped up near the rock. This one had red-gold hair. She looked at Rommy, and there was a curiosity in her golden eyes rather than the coldness Rommy had seen in the dark-haired ones'. This mermaid smiled tentatively, and Rommy found herself smiling back even as she remembered Finn's warning.

"Alice, come away from the water's edge," Rommy said. The little girl, fascinated with the mermaids, had been edging toward the shoreline. The blonde mermaid was beckoning her playfully.

"I want to play with the fish girls," said Alice. "They aren't nearly as scary as Danny and his boys."

"You can't play with mermaids, Alice," Finn said. "Not ever."

Alice made a face and plopped down in the sand.

She picked up a small pebble and threw it into the water, but she stayed put. Rommy sighed with relief and turned back to Finn.

"Look, I need to check things out," Finn said. "You and Alice can stay here until I get back. Just be sure neither of you go near the water."

"Wouldn't it be better if we went with you?" Rommy asked, glancing nervously at the lagoon. She hoped those mermaids couldn't come out onto the beach at all.

"It's safer here," said Finn. "Plus, I can go faster if you two stay here. I'll be back before you even know it."

Rommy didn't like it, but what choice did she have? While she didn't fully trust Finn, in this strange world where mermaids wanted to drown you, it seemed safer to wait for him to guide them. She just hoped he wouldn't be gone long.

She looked around the beach. The only way out was to climb up over the cliffs. Then, with a start, she remembered that she and Alice could still fly here.

"All right," she said. "We'll wait here, but if you're not back in an hour, we're going to look for my father. That's why I'm here, after all. As interesting as all this is," she motioned toward the blonde and redheaded mermaids playing in the water, "it isn't why I came."

"I won't be long," said Finn, pushing off the sand into the air.

17
THE BETRAYAL

Rommy watched Finn fly off with an uneasy feeling. A splashing noise drew her attention. Alice had moved to the water's edge and was wading through the shallows up to her ankles. Rommy spotted the blonde-headed mermaid coming closer.

She rushed up to Alice and yanked her away from the water. Alice threw her a dirty look. "It wasn't like I was going in. I was just staying at the edges like."

"I don't know how close they can come, Alice," said Rommy. "I don't think I could save you if they pulled you in, and neither of us can breathe underwater, even if we can fly." Rommy shuddered at the idea of being dragged into the beautiful, turquoise waters and never coming up again.

Alice kicked a few pebbles into the water in protest, but she wandered further up the beach. Rommy walked to a cluster of rocks and sat on the biggest one. A small tidal pool had formed between the rocks, and she stared into it fascinated by the minuscule creatures flittering just under the surface. Idly, she wondered what happened to them. Did the tide come in and carry them back out or did the pool dry up? Would the creatures be left gasping on the pink sand like a fish out of water?

Rommy shook her head at her morbid thoughts and studied the area. Cliffs sheltered the beach on three sides. A tangle of vines and flowers crawled over the sides of the cliffs, and large bushes grew at their base. Their flowers were huge and a deep red color, almost like blood. As she watched, a small emerald bird flew near the crimson blooms. It flitted in and out of the vines.

Rommy checked on Alice and found she was playing in another small tidal pool. Satisfied that she was away from the water's edge and the mermaids, Rommy moved closer to the flowers. They appeared to be undulating. The bird was zipping in and out of the vines. Rommy guessed it was looking for bugs.

"They're pretty, but I wouldn't get too close if I were you," said a voice near her ear.

Rommy whirled around. A boy about her own age or maybe a little younger was hovering in the air.

She hadn't heard him at all. He had nut-brown hair and eyes that matched. A puckish grin spread across his face.

With strange light in his eyes, he pointed his finger. "Just watch."

Rommy turned back to the flowers just in time to see one of the beautiful blossoms appear to lunge up and out. The bird disappeared into the mouth of the bloom which had closed. The flower's closed petals bulged as its victim tried to escape. It didn't take long for the struggling to stop.

The boy hooted with laughter. "Those zippits never learn."

Rommy shivered. "That's horrible! That poor bird."

The boy shrugged. "You play, you pay." He flew in a quick loop. "It's the circle of life." He laughed again.

Alice came skipping over to them. "Who are you?" she asked.

Rommy had been wondering the same thing, but leave it to Alice to just ask outright.

"You mean you've come to Neverland and you don't know who I am?" The boy's wood brown eyes should have been warm, but somehow they weren't at all. There was a hard glitter to them that made Rommy pull Alice closer to her.

The boy smiled and made a bow mid-air. "Then,

allow me to introduce myself. My name is Pan. Peter Pan."

"Peter Pan!" said Alice, wonder in her voice. "The boys talk about you all the time. Danny would be pea green with jealousy if he knew I'd met you! He wants to be a Lost Boy ever so much!"

Pan flew until he hovered cross-legged in front of Alice. "So, the boys talk about me do they? What do they say?"

"Well, they think you're a right smart one all right. I heard Danny bragging to the other boys you sneaked into one of the toff's houses and come out with his youngest boy."

"What do you mean, Alice?" Rommy asked sharply.

Before Alice could answer, Pan had taken Alice's hands and pulled her into the air, twirling her around until she giggled. "And what about you?" asked Pan. "Did you come here to be a Lost Boy?"

Alice raised an eyebrow. "I can't be a Lost Boy. I'm a girl."

Pan swirled them back down to the spun sugar sand and puffed out his chest. "I'll let you join us even if you are a girl. After all, I decide who joins us and who doesn't."

He whirled and Rommy found herself almost nose to nose with him. "And who are you?"

Straightening her shoulders, she said, "My name is Rommy."

"Rommy, hmm? What are you doing here?"

Rommy didn't know if she should mention Finn or not, so she stuck with the shortest answer. "I came to find my father."

Pan hooted with laughter again. "Grown-ups don't come to Neverland! Boy are you dumb!"

Alice put her hands on her hips. "That's what you know! Finn said Rommy's Papa was here. He's a sea captain."

Rommy looked at Alice and gave a slight shake of her head.

Pan's laughter cut off. "A sea captain you say? How long has he been in Neverland?"

"I'm not sure," said Rommy. "He wasn't where he was supposed to be, so I came looking for him."

"Grown-ups never do what they say," said Pan. He grinned, and Rommy noticed she could see quite a lot of his small, pointed teeth.

Rommy felt Alice grip her hand.

"Pan!" a voice called.

Rommy let out a breath she hadn't realized she'd been holding. Pan flew up to meet Finn as Finn made his way over the cliffs. "When did you get back?" Pan asked.

"I just arrived," said Finn. "I wanted to scout things out before I went bumbling into an ambush."

Finn's voice was casual, but Rommy saw his eyes darting between her and Pan.

"I see you brought new friends," said Pan, gesturing toward them.

Finn shrugged. "I thought you'd be happy to meet them both."

"I was delighted," said Pan. "Alice will make an excellent Lost Boy even if she is a girl, and I was just talking to Rommy about her father." He paused. "The sea captain."

The two boys landed on the beach. Rommy and Alice stood a short distance away. Something was going on here. She didn't know what exactly, but she didn't like it. Alice must have noticed it too because she moved closer to Rommy.

Finn forced a laugh. "I see you figured it out with no one having to tell you." He clapped Pan on the back. "I'm sure Captain Hook will be surprised to see his daughter."

Pan grinned again, baring his teeth. "I'm sure he will. I know I was."

Rommy stepped forward. "Captain Hook? I'm afraid you've made a big mistake. Our last name is Cavendish, not Hook." She glared at Finn. "I told you he wasn't here."

Finn refused to meet her eyes but kept on smiling at Pan.

Pan hooted again. "Oh, that's not his last name. They call him that because of this!" Pan balled his hand into a fist and then curled his index finger. "He's the most notorious pirate in Neverland. He and his men are floating out in the Cove right now."

A block of ice formed in Rommy's stomach. Papa couldn't be a pirate. Could he?

She shook her head. "You're mistaken. There has to be another explanation."

"Your father is missing his left hand isn't he?" said Finn, meeting her eyes for the first time. "He has a silver hook doesn't he?"

"Yes, but... but he can't be a pirate," she said. "He would have told me."

Pan stepped closer to her. "I told you. You can't ever trust grown-ups. They lie and disappoint you."

Rommy pushed her lips together to stop their quivering and lifted her chin. "I don't believe you, either of you," she said firmly. "I don't know what's going on here or what you are up to, but my Papa doesn't lie. At least not to me."

Pan shrugged. "Believe me or not. You'll see what your Papa is soon enough." He nodded at Finn. "Good work bringing her here."

"What does he mean?" Rommy looked at Finn, the pieces beginning to fall into place.

"You don't think it was a coincidence I just showed up do you?" Finn smirked. "Captain Hook laid siege to our hideout. I wasn't there when it happened. When I realized what was going on, I came to find you. You just made my job easier when you left that fancy boarding school of yours. I wasn't sure how I'd get you out of there without raising an alarm."

Pan put his arm around Finn's shoulder. There was an edge to his voice. "You kept this close to the vest. I had no idea Hook had a daughter."

Finn shrugged again, dislodging Pan's arm. "I knew she'd come in handy one day."

Rommy's heart dropped. Her last link with London snapped with an almost audible click. She had started to trust Finn, thought they were friends of a sort, but he'd been lying to her all along. Angry tears sprang into her eyes.

Pan crowed. "Oh-ho, did you think you were friends?"

"You toe rag!" yelled Alice, rushing to Finn and kicking him hard in the shin. Using her small fists, she pummeled his stomach. He grabbed her hands. "Stop it now, Alice."

Alice fought him, trying to pull away and continuing to kick at him.

Pan laughed. "She'll fit right in with the Lost Boys! Let's go. I'll take Miss Alice." He swooped down and scooped the little girl into a tight hug against his body so she couldn't kick or hit him.

"You bring the Captain's daughter," Pan nodded to Finn. "We'll stay in the caves on the other side of the Indian camp for now. We can't go back to the hideout." He looked at Rommy. "Your father blew that all to smithereens."

Rommy lifted her chin and glared at both Pan and Finn. Finn met her gaze. "Come on then or do I have to wrap you up like Alice?"

Instead of answering, Rommy sprang into the air and followed Pan.

18

THE CAPTURE

The small group flew up over the cliffs. As they cleared the top, a vast jungle stretched out underneath them. Rommy could see the enormous trees swaying and moving although she couldn't see what was causing the movement.

They flew on until the jungle thinned out, and the ground dropped away again. Down they swooped following a large tumbling river as it rushed over another cliff forming a waterfall. At the base of the waterfall were a series of caves. Pan landed inside one and set Alice on the ground. She immediately moved away from him. Rommy landed next to the little girl who pushed herself into Rommy's side. Finn landed just behind them.

The cave opening was narrow, but once inside, it opened into a large cavern. Natural rock formations formed shelves of sorts along the walls. At various places, roots from the trees above had snaked through the crevices in the rock, tangling along the top of the cavern. Stretched between several of these roots was what looked like a giant woven sack with an opening along the side.

Finn looked around. "I'll get stuff to make more beds."

Late afternoon had given way to twilight, but the cave's far reaches were cloaked in dark shadows. Rommy put her arms around Alice. The little girl was shivering. She didn't know if Alice was cold or afraid. Probably both at this point. She looked around, assessing. Her mind was already churning with ways to get away from Pan and Finn. If her father was here, she would find him. Then they could all go back to London, back to normal life and away from this place where flowers ate birds.

Pan smiled knowingly. "Don't think about leaving. Wandering around here at night is not a wise decision. Those flowers are nothing compared to what's out there that would welcome you both as a snack."

Rommy lifted her chin. "The worst monster seems to be in here. Not out there."

"Why am I the monster?" Pan asked in an injured tone. "Am I the one who laid siege to a group of motherless boys? Am I the one who broke into their home - the only home they knew - and blew it to smithereens? Am I the one who took those same motherless boys, and even now is threatening to make them walk the plank?"

Pan slid next to her and put his hand on Alice's head. "I'm trying to help my boys. I take care of them. Where would they be without me and Neverland? I'd tell you - out on the streets of London, starving or worse. I'm not the monster here." He ruffled Alice's hair, and she shrank back against Rommy. "I just want my boys back, and you can help me."

Rommy glared at him. "Papa would never hurt children. You're lying!"

"You are boringly repetitive. Why would I lie? The truth is your father has been hunting me for years. He just showed up one day, and he made it his mission to get rid of me."

"That doesn't make any sense. Why would my father come here, of all places, to hunt you down? We have land in the St. Croix, and he was a wealthy man with a business to run. Why would he leave all that and come to a place like this?"

"That is the question, isn't it?" said Pan, rubbing his chin.

"Maybe you stole something from him," piped up Alice. "You know, like that toff's boy."

Rommy stared at Alice. "What?"

"I said, maybe he stole something from your old man, something that was worth a whole lot."

Rommy looked up at Pan. "Is that true?"

Pan shrugged. "I never saw Hook before he came here."

"Even if this Hook is my father, he would never hurt children," Rommy said stubbornly. "You're just trying to gain my sympathy."

"No, it's true," said Finn, coming in with a bundle of branches and vines in his arms. Several small balls of light buzzed around his head. He plopped onto the cave floor and began twisting and braiding the tangle of vegetation. The fairies wove in and out. Rommy wasn't sure if they were helping or playing.

"Why should I believe anything you say?" asked Rommy. "You've been lying to me since London, and who knows how long you were spying on me before that." A thought made her stop. "Were you in my school?"

"You should thank me. If I hadn't lured her into that other part of the building, that yellow-haired girl would have gotten you into trouble. As it was, I distracted the old lady and kept that girl from causing problems."

"It was you that slammed that door wasn't it?" Rommy swallowed. Chattingham's seemed very far away, and she wondered what had happened to Primrose and how Francie was getting along. Had they found out she was gone yet?

Finn nodded. "That would have been me. You can thank me for keeping you and your friend out of trouble." He chuckled. "That girl had a lot of explaining to do."

"I'll thank you for nothing," said Rommy. "You tricked me and brought me here. My father probably isn't even here at all, and now I'm stuck and Alice too!"

Alice patted Rommy's arm. "It's all right. If you hadn't come along, Danny would have messed me over but good."

Rommy hugged the little girl to her. "I'm still sorry that I dragged you into all this."

She looked up at Pan and Finn who were finishing up several more of the woven contraptions. The fairies lifted the creations into the air and hung them on the roots along the curving roof of the cave.

"I'm hungry," said Alice as her stomach made a loud rumbling noise. Rommy hadn't even noticed her own hunger until Alice said something. Thinking back, she realized the last thing she had eaten was the apple in the railway station. That had been early this morning. Now the sun had set, and it was dark outside the cave entrance.

"Why should we feed either of you?" Pan asked. "Maybe it would be better to keep you weak and hungry, so you aren't stupid enough to try to escape."

"Come on, Pan," said Finn. "The little girl needs to eat."

He walked over to a sack at the back of the cave

and rummaged around. He took two bundles and shoved them both into Rommy's hands. "Here, this should hold you until we can hunt in the morning," he said.

Before Rommy's hands could close over the bundles, Pan had zipped between them, snatching both away from her. "Hey!" she yelled at him.

Pan flipped over on his back and unwrapped the food. "Cheese and bread! How delicious!" He took a large bite from the bread and chewed noisily.

"Knock it off, Pan," said Finn. His jaw clenched tightly.

Pan was suddenly in his face. "What did you say to me?"

Finn didn't back down, but he moderated the irritation out of his voice. "I just mean it won't hurt to give them some food. I, for one, don't want to listen to them whining all night long about being hungry."

Pan eyed Rommy and Alice. He flew a lazy circle around them both. "Well, what do you think? Should I feed you both? Or maybe just one of you?" He laughed and crammed more bread into his mouth.

Alice narrowed her eyes, but she said nothing.

Pan flew up close to her. "Don't you like that idea, Lost Girl?" He patted her on the head and she swatted his hand away. Pan laughed. "I like you. I really do." He broke off a small piece of the bread and another piece of cheese and gave them to her.

"What about Rommy?" said Alice. "She's hungry too!"

"The question is, how hungry?" Pan circled Rommy. She worked at keeping her face serene and not moving, but it was hard. He slithered around her like a snake. He hovered mid-air with his cheek next to hers. Rommy had to fight the urge to pull away from him. He leaned even closer and whispered in her ear, "I rather like you, too."

Then he flew up and let out a loud crowing laugh. "But I don't like you enough to share this!" He stuffed the rest of the bread and cheese into his mouth.

"Why.. Why.." Alice clenched her fists, crushing the food she was holding.

Rommy put her hand on the little girl's shoulder. "Don't," she said. Alice looked at her with wide eyes. "But, but.."

Rommy shook her head. Her eyes never left Pan who was still circling overhead. "Eat your food, Alice," she said quietly.

Alice looked from her to Pan and back again. Slowly, she brought the bread up to her mouth and began to chew. The silence stretched out as Alice finished the bread and cheese.

Finn broke the tension. "I'm tired," he said. "Don't we have to get up early, Pan? Maybe we should all turn in?"

Before Pan could reply, Alice yawned widely. He

pointed at them. "You both get into your beds now, so I can see you."

Rommy and Alice pushed off from the floor and floated toward the two sleeping sacks that hung toward the back of the cave. Though Rommy's stomach was uncomfortably empty, tiredness wash over her as Alice squirmed into her sleeping quarters. Waking up to Francie staring at her seemed days ago.

Pan floated up beside Rommy "Remember what I said. If you leave here, you and Alice won't survive the night. I'd hate to see Alice pay any more for your foolishness. Besides, tomorrow you and your father can be reunited - at least for a little while." Pan's smile was cold.

Rommy didn't answer but made her way into her own bed. She slid into the opening and found the inside surprisingly comfortable for something made of branches and vines.

From her perch she could see out the cave entrance. A lavender moon was shining and what looked like a million stars, each one twinkling with a different pastel light.

Alice's voice floated through the air. "Night, Rommy!"

"Goodnight, Alice."

Rommy stared at the moon. Its strange color in the midnight sky reminded her of how very far from home she was. Was her father really here? And if he was, why? Could he really be somebody completely different from the father she'd known her whole life? It seemed impossible to her.

Despite her empty stomach, the hurt of Finn's betrayal and her worry about what was going on, Rommy's eyelids grew heavy. She tried to keep them open, but the gentle rocking of the hammock lulled her toward sleep.

19
THE RISK

"Rommy, Rommy." The voice intruded into her sleep. A small hand pulled at her, jostling her rudely.

"Tired," she mumbled. "Go away, Francie." She tried to push away from the voice and the hand.

A small head poked into the hammock opening and hissed louder this time. "Rommy! It's Alice! Wake up!"

Rommy blinked her eyes a few times and tried to sit up, but her bed was moving. A small figure crowded into the opening. A pair of violet blue eyes peered up into her face. Rommy shook her head and took in her surroundings. It was dark but a sliver of lavender moon faintly illuminated the inside of the cave.

It all came flooding back. Her Papa missing. Her mad flight to Neverland.

Finn's betrayal.

Pan's menace.

"Alice, what are you doing? Are you frightened?"

"We should both be frightened. That Pan fellow is off his chump for sure. We need to hook it."

"Alice, I'd like nothing more than to get away from them both, and I agree. Pan isn't, well, there is something not quite right about him. But even if my father is here, I don't know where he is. We can't go wandering around this island. There are flowers that eat things and mermaids that want to drown people. I don't want to end up in a worse situation or drag you into anymore danger."

"It's better to take our chances out there. Staying here is a bad idea. I know it here." Alice pointed to her chest. Fear was etched on Alice's face, and fear wasn't something Rommy equated to the little girl.

"You really think it's worse to stay than to leave?" Rommy asked. Alice nodded vigorously. Rommy poked her head out of the opening and looked around. The bottom of Pan's hammock was visible, and a bare leg hung out of the opening. She craned her head and spotted Finn's sleep sack. It swung gently, but there was no sign of him. A dim light glowed through the sides. The fairies must be in there with him, Rommy realized. The boys' beds hung between theirs and the entrance.

She pulled her head back. "We must be very, very quiet." Alice nodded solemnly.

Rommy slipped out of the hammock first and looked around in the gloom. She stared at Pan's hammock and then Finn's, straining her ears for any sounds of movement. After a moment, she beckoned to Alice. The little girl slid soundlessly from the opening. The two girls glided out of the cave and into the moonlit night.

Once outside, they flew a little ways and then stopped. Rommy had no idea where they should go now. "Maybe we should hide somewhere until its morning," she said.

"We need to get far away from that bloke." Alice jerked a thumb over her shoulder toward the cave. "Maybe we can hide in the jungle."

Rommy shook her head. "I think we should stay away from there, especially at nighttime." She twisted around, her mind scrambling to come up with a plan. The glint of moon on water sparked an idea. "Maybe we can follow that river, and it will lead to my father's ship. If he's even here, that is."

Alice shrugged. "Sounds good as long as it's away from that crazy Pan fellow."

The two girls turned and followed the river until they were out of sight from the cave entrance and then touched down. As she landed in the grassy river bank, it hit Rommy that she didn't even think twice about flying now. How odd that was.

"Why are we landing? Shouldn't we bunk it as far as we can?" Alice asked.

"I just want to get my bearings," said Rommy. "I don't want anyone, or any*thing*, I guess, to spot us, but I don't want to go into the trees because we can't be sure what sorts of things live in there. Let's walk for a while. We might be less conspicuous that way."

The girls walked beside the riverbank, trying to stay close but not actually in the tall grasses that grew along the water's edge. Rommy wasn't sure what deadly creatures, or even plants, this island held. The moon's pale purple light made it easy to follow the path as the two trudged on.

A rustling sound made both girls freeze. Rommy craned her neck, trying to identify what had made the noise. Silence surrounded them. She had just decided to keep going when Alice's eyes got wide. She put a small hand on Rommy's arm and pulled as she shot toward the sky, gasping, "F.. f.. fly!"

Rommy heard the heavy slither and rustle at the same moment and launched herself skyward. She heard heavy jaws clack together and felt hot breath on her right foot. She looked down and a huge beast, covered in scales, its snout pointed toward the air, snapped its mammoth jaws several times in quick succession. It let out a bellow that rumbled through Rommy's body.

Alice grasped her hand as the two flew away from the creature as fast as they could. "Crikey! That was close. We were almost done for. What was it?"

Rommy shook her head, and her voice was

unsteady when she answered. "I'm not sure. We've studied animals in science class. I think it was some type of reptile. Whatever it was, I don't want to get a closer look. I think we should stay in the air though."

Alice gave a dramatic shiver. "I hope there's nothing like that thing that flies."

Rommy hoped so, too.

The girls flew onward, following the river that flowed beneath them. After what seemed like miles, Rommy looked over at Alice. She had to be getting tired because Rommy could feel the weight of weariness on her own body. The adrenaline of escaping and then their close encounter with the creature had worn off, and Rommy thought she would give anything for her bed at Chattingham's.

Still they flew on, following the river as it snaked and twisted, the banks getting rockier and steeper. Alice started to fall behind, looking half asleep. She gamely tried to keep up, putting on short bursts of speed to catch up.

Around the curve in the river, Rommy spotted a single weeping willow tree. She thought it looked like a good place to rest. Besides, it was clear Alice wouldn't last much longer. Rommy flew around the tree, checking to be sure nothing was in its branches. Then she gestured to Alice, and the two alighted on one of its thick branches.

Alice sighed. "I don't mind saying it. My flying

muscles are plum wore out." Her shoulders drooped.

"I'm tired, too. Let's rest a bit before we go on."

Rommy settled herself on the wide branch with her back to the thick trunk. Alice curled up next to her; her eyelids drifting closed almost immediately. Rommy grabbed a section of the girl's dress in her hand, afraid Alice would fall out of the tree. She leaned her head back against the trunk and tried to think of what to do next.

They couldn't stay here, but they had to sleep. She was tired and Alice was only six. She couldn't walk or fly forever. Rommy sighed. It had probably been a mistake to leave. She wasn't sure where she was going, and if Pan and Finn woke up, they had a big advantage. She'd lay bets they both knew this island like the back of their hands.

Rommy felt the prickle of tears and tried to blink them back. It seemed like a hundred years ago that she was waiting in the visiting parlor at Chattingham's, wondering why Papa was late.

She gave a small hiccupy laugh. Her father couldn't say she wasn't able to take care of herself now. That is, if she got out of this in one piece and Alice with her.

Rommy glanced down at the little girl. Sleep made her look young. She was a pretty child with a china doll's features and soft black hair that ended in curls. Rommy hated to think of what might happen to Alice if she returned to the streets. She determined that if–no when–she found Papa, she would persuade him to take in Alice. They had the money for one more small girl.

The moon was setting, and the stars were—it couldn't be—but they seemed to be singing. Rommy blinked her eyes a few times, thinking she had fallen asleep and was dreaming. But no, the stars were giving off a hauntingly beautiful melody.

She wondered what Francie was doing now. She was probably frantic with worry. Rommy hoped she wouldn't get into too much trouble. There would be no chance of Francie covering for her for another whole day, if she even got back then.

Rommy shut her eyes. Just for a moment, she told herself.

20
THE CAMP

A low yelp startled Rommy awake. She tried to leap to her feet but found branches weren't a great place to do that. She caught her balance against the ancient trunk of the tree and felt twigs snagging into her hair.

Dawn was just creeping into the sky, and there were still shadows within the branches of the big tree. One of those shadows moved. A large man stood. He had bronze-colored skin and black hair, and in one of his arms, he held Alice. He was shaking his other hand, and Rommy thought she saw blood on it.

Alice was kicking her legs and squirming so much Rommy was reluctantly impressed that the big man could keep a hold of her. She started forward to help Alice, but a pair of large arms surrounded her in a suffocating bear hug.

For a moment, panic paralyzed Rommy. The man took the opportunity to sling her over his shoulder. She felt a sharp pain in her scalp as her hair caught on a twig and her braid came loose in a clatter of bobby pins. The pain startled Rommy back to life. She squirmed to get loose and kicked her feet. The man's arm tightened around her middle until her ribs creaked. She was jostled nearly breathless as the man climbed down the tree.

Once on the ground, he didn't set her down but continued down a faint path next to the river. Rommy used her fists to hit him, but it was like striking a stone. By now, her breath was coming in gasps. She tried to lift her head but didn't get very far with a band of solid muscle holding her in place. She could hear Alice yelling to be put her down. The man who had grabbed Alice didn't respond except for the occasional grunt.

Rommy tried to twist to one side to see where they were going, but the back she was bouncing against was so broad, she couldn't glimpse anything else. The only things visible were the fawn-colored trousers the man wore and his soft looking shoes.

Rommy finally stilled, so she could catch her breath. She just hoped it wasn't very far to where they were going because hanging upside down was decidedly unpleasant, and her head was aching from all the bouncing. Alice's voice drifted toward her, calling the other man a toe rag and a few other words Rommy had never heard before.

It seemed to take forever but probably wasn't more than ten minutes before the man stopped, and Rommy's world swung right side up again. It took a moment for things to stop spinning. When it did, she found herself standing in a small encampment.

A ring of tall, conical tents were pitched around a large fire pit where an old woman was cooking something. A girl a little older than Rommy stood in front of one of the tents. Her arms were crossed, and a long black braid hung to her waist. She wore a fierce expression, and her black eyes snapped as they raked over Rommy and then Alice.

"Who are these English and why did you bring them here, Wolf?" She addressed the man that had been holding Rommy.

"We saw them up a tree when we were out scouting. They did not seem to belong."

Rommy looked around, looking for an escape route. The large man was still holding Alice, trying to keep her from kicking and biting him. Rommy stepped back but found her captor standing there like a brick wall. One of his large hands came down on her shoulder.

"The little one does not seem too happy to be here, Little Bear," the old woman said chuckling. She got up slowly and walked closer to the big man holding Alice.

"No, she is not," Little Bear answered in what was an obvious understatement.

"What is your name, little one?" she asked as she got closer.

Rommy saw Alice screw up her face and lift her chin. "Who wants to know?"

The woman let out a soft laugh. "Ah, I see we have a fierce little warrior princess here. You must calm yourself, child. We will not hurt you or your sister."

Alice stopped kicking and looked at the old woman. "You gots a funny way of showing it." Alice jerked a thumb in Rommy's direction. "She ain't my sister, but she saved me. What's your name?"

The woman smiled kindly. "My name is Little Owl." She turned to scrutinize Rommy and then looked back at Alice. "That sounds like a story I want to hear, about how this young girl saved you. We don't often get English girls here. I can only remember one during my time, but she left a long time ago."

While the woman was talking, one of the tent flaps opened, and a tall man ducked through the opening and came to stand by Little Owl. He had black hair threaded with silver that hung in a straight sheet past his shoulders. "Mother, who are our guests?"

Little Owl shrugged her shoulders. "They have not shared their names yet."

Little Bear had cautiously put Alice on the ground, but still kept his big hands on her shoulders. Alice shrugged them off and came to stand in front of the tall, older man. "We ain't guests. They took us right out of a tree and brought us here without a by your leave!"

"Oh ho, is that right, little one. I am sorry about your abrupt invitation, but you are now our guests. Please come and sit by the fire. Mother will have breakfast ready soon."

He turned to look at the fierce girl who was still glaring at Rommy. "Tiger Lily, come help your grand-mother to welcome our guests." The girl moved reluctantly to help the older woman prepare the meal, but she kept darting hostile looks at them.

The older man turned and looked at Rommy and Alice. "I am Chief Hawk Eye. We still have not the pleasure of your names."

Alice put a thumb to her chest. "My name is Alice, and that's Rommy," she said, pointing in Rommy's direction.

"Rommy, Alice, please come sit by the fire." The older man gestured toward several rocks gathered around the fire pit that served as seats. Rommy grasped Alice's hand, and they sat down. After the night out, the warmth felt good, and whatever was cooking made Rommy's mouth water. She'd had little eat, and besides the bit of bread and cheese Pan had given Alice, she didn't know what the little girl's last meal had been. She guessed it hadn't been much, whatever it was.

As if in answer to Rommy's thoughts, Alice's stomach rumbled loudly. Little Owl chuckled again. "We'll have food for you soon, little Alice." She gently smoothed a hand over Alice's tangled hair, and Alice gave her a dimpled grin.

It didn't take long for Little Owl to finish cooking breakfast, and Rommy soon found herself with a roasted fish wrapped in leaves on her lap.

Rommy unwrapped her fish and broke off small pieces to eat. Alice didn't wait. She immediately began devouring her meal. The old woman seemed particularly delighted with Alice and laughed at the little girl's enthusiasm.

"Now you must tell us this story," Little Owl said. She turned to the chief. "Alice told us that Rommy is not her sister, but she saved Alice."

The chief gave Rommy a long look. "You are so quiet and still, but sometimes the best warriors are so. Tell us." He looked at the girls expectantly.

Alice, having finished her fish, wiped her mouth with the sleeve of her dress. She then launched into a spirited retelling of Rommy charging down the alley and taking on the five boys.

"You should have seen her," said Alice. "She leaped on top of this crate and she knocked Danny on his bum. His two boys came at her, and bam, she knocked one into the other, and they both went down in a giant ball of arms and legs. I thought she was going to win, but that toe rag Danny grabbed her ankle. Twern't fair fighting, and once Danny was sitting on her, well, you couldn't move that bull no way, no how. That's when Finn came and knocked Danny into next week." Alice leaned over and threw her arms around Rommy. "But if Rommy hadn't come when she did, I don't like to think of the thrashing Danny would have given me. I'd been lucky to have come out with all my teeth and able to walk, I would have."

Little Bear gave a low growl. "Who is this Danny person? What big boy beats up a little girl?" He gave a snort of disgust.

Tiger Lily had been eyeing Rommy skeptically as Alice told the story. "A small girl like you almost bested five large boys? I think Alice is telling us a tall tale." She flipped her braid over her shoulder.

"No, I'm not!" exclaimed Alice indignantly. "I'm telling the honest to goodness truth. Rommy used this piece of wood like a sword." Leaping up, Alice grabbed a stick. She jumped onto a rock and thrust the stick back and forth. "It was like she was dancing. She whirled and twirled. She may be kind of puny, but if you give her a sword, our Rommy's dangerous." Alice said this like it was the best thing in the world.

Rommy tucked a strand of loose hair behind her ear and shrugged, her cheeks heating. "Well, I didn't best them all. Finn had to help us. Although he ended up not being much help in the end, did he?"

The chief drew his head back, frowning. "Young Finn is a good boy. He watches out for the littlest Lost Boys and protects them from some of Pan's mad schemes."

Tiger Lily leaped to her feet. "Peter's schemes aren't mad. He's just been hounded by that horrible Captain Hook. Can you blame him for trying to come up with a plan to get rid of him?"

Alice opened her mouth, but Rommy nudged her with an elbow. "I don't want to get involved in any of the fights on this island. What I want to do is to get to the Cove."

Little Owl frowned. "Why would you want to do that, child? There are pirates down there. Young girls like you should stay away from Captain Hook and his crew. It would be too dangerous."

"Because when you are Hook's daughter, he isn't dangerous at all. Isn't that right, Rommy?" came a voice above their heads.

An icy hand squeezed her heart even as Alice's small, sweaty one squeezed her arm. Pan was circling over their heads, and Finn was with him.

21
THE VOTE

Four pairs of dark eyes stared at Rommy. Tiger Lily only had eyes for Pan. The fierce look on her face melted into a smile that changed her whole appearance.

Finally, the chief spoke into the loud silence. "Is this true? Is your father Captain Hook?" His black eyes pierced into Rommy's hazel ones. She stared back for a long moment.

"I.. I don't know," she said.

"What do you mean, you don't know?" the chief asked. "How can you not know who your father is?"

Rommy felt the sting of tears again and blinked several times. "I thought I did know, but now…" She looked around helplessly, trying to find an answer to a question that would have been obvious only a few days ago.

The group around the fire pit, with the exception

of Tiger Lily, were looking at her with a mixture of pity and anger. Pan, on the other hand, appeared to be having a marvelous time. A sly grin was on his face and his whole body was leaning forward as if watching a favorite play. Finn wasn't smiling though. In fact, if Rommy didn't know better, the look Finn gave Pan was anything but friendly.

Little Owl finally broke the frozen tableau around the fire. She walked over to Rommy and laid her old, gnarled hands softly on her shoulders. "Child, why did you come here to Neverland? You are obviously well-born. I can hear it in your speech, and yet, here you are with little Alice who is not so gently born, I think. It is time you told your story."

The gentleness of Little Owl's voice and the kindness in her eyes almost undid Rommy. It had been a long few days, but she took a deep breath. Tears would not help this situation, and she wouldn't give Pan the satisfaction. The thought of Pan gave her a steely determination. She squared her shoulders and lifted her chin to look right into Little Owl's eyes.

"My father always comes to my school for my birthday. I only see him twice a year, and my birthday is one of those days. He's never missed it. Ever. But this year he didn't come. Everyone told me he was delayed and that these things happened, but I could tell they didn't truly believe that." Rommy stopped and looked around at the group listening. "I waited the entire next day, but Papa never showed up and he didn't send any messages. I knew I had to do something, so I sneaked out of my school. My friend Francie helped me, and she was going to cover for me so nobody knew I was gone. Then, I went to my father's offices. I thought I could find out something there. It was on the way there that I ran into Alice and Finn. But when we got to the offices, they were empty."

Rommy paused and swallowed. Little Owl waited patiently as Rommy gathered her composure again.

"Not just empty. It looked like nobody had been there in a long time. Years. That's when Finn offered to take me here." She looked back at the boy who was staring at his feet.

"But it was just a trick. He brought me here so Peter Pan could use me to somehow get at Captain Hook. I don't know if this Hook is my father or not, but from what I've heard, he is far different from the Papa I know." Rommy's voice dropped to a whisper so only Little Owl could hear her. "If Papa is Captain Hook, then he's been lying my whole life, and I don't know him. At all." She turned her head as several tears slipped out against her will.

Little Owl turned Rommy's face back to hers and smiled. "Still waters indeed," she said. "Well, you have nothing of the look of Captain Hook or his temperament. It is only your skills with a sword that connect you, but we only have little Alice's word for that."

"I look like my mother," said Rommy. "She died when I was born, but I've been told I am her mirror image."

The chief stepped forward and directed his words toward Finn. "Why did you bring her here? Why did you think she was Hook's daughter?"

Finn straightened from where he had been slouching against a rock. "I followed Captain Hook, sir. I followed him one time when he went to visit her. That's why I'm sure she's Hook's daughter. I've seen them together. I thought, well, I thought it was a good thing to learn about Hook, and that turned out to be true."

Rommy drew in a sharp breath. The idea that Finn had been watching her, not just in recent days, but for a long time made a knot form in her stomach. He had been there all along and she hadn't known. Apparently, there was a lot she didn't know. The life she assumed she had was a big hoax. Was anything true anymore?

"All this chatter is great fun," said Pan, "but we need to rescue the Lost Boys." He flew down to stand between Rommy and Alice. Finn moved to the other side of Rommy.

"What do you plan to do with these girls?" the chief asked.

"They are the bait for our trap," answered Pan,

the glee in his voice unmistakable now. "At least she is." He nodded toward Rommy. "Alice can be one of the Lost Boys. She has the spirit for it, and it doesn't sound like she has anything to go back to, anyway." Pan shrugged carelessly.

Alice glared up at him. "Sure, don't ask me what I want. Who am I to have a say in what happens to me?" She crossed her arms.

Tiger Lily scowled at Alice. "You should be glad he wants you. Nobody else seems to care. And what does it matter what Peter does with her?" she said gesturing to Rommy. "Hook is our enemy. He's always been our enemy. He tried to kill me to get Peter. Turn about is fair play."

Rommy stepped forward until she was standing in front of Alice. "I don't care how you feel about me. In fact, I can see how you might despise me if this Hook is as bad as you say, and you think I'm his daughter. But Alice has done nothing to you, so stop being so nasty to her. Of course she should get a say in what happens to her. Keeping her here as a Lost Boy is the same as keeping her prisoner. That's hardly fair since she has nothing to do with any of this."

Tiger Lily's eyes snapped, and she opened her mouth, but her father put up his hand. "Daughter, I am ashamed of you. Little Alice has done nothing to you that you should be so unkind, and young

Rommy seems to be as much a victim in all this as Alice."

He turned to Finn. "You'd put these girls in danger for your own ends?"

"Sir, with all due respect, Captain Hook has all the Lost Boys, even little Walter. He's threatening to make them all walk the plank if Pan doesn't deliver himself tied up like a Christmas present. His daughter might be the only thing we have to save them and keep Peter from his clutches."

The chief turned solemn dark eyes on Pan. "You would save yourself at the expense of your boys?"

Pan laughed. "Why do I need to sacrifice myself when Hook's daughter has presented herself as an answer to all my problems? She doesn't even have to get hurt. All we need her for is to lure him off that ship. Once he's off the ship, he's easy pickings."

"Yes, why should he when he has Hook's daughter to use?" Tiger Lily demanded, glaring at her father.

"Daughter, be silent!" the chief thundered. Silence stretched over the group. In a softer voice the chief said, "I will talk this over with my people."

The group withdrew. Rommy could hear the rise and fall of their voices. One voice - she thought it was the one called Wolf - rose louder. "This isn't our concern. Just give them to Pan and be done with it. Hook is our common enemy, and we need Pan and

the Lost Boys as our allies. It was Pan who saved
Tiger Lily, after all."

Rommy heard Little Owl respond, but she
couldn't make out what she was saying. Pan looked
at her through slitted eyes, a large grin on his face.
"They'll turn you over to me, don't worry," he said.
"Tiger Lily will persuade them."

Rommy ignored him, and when Alice put her
hands on her hips and opened her mouth, she put a
hand on the little girl's shoulder. Alice closed her
mouth again, but she continued to glare at Pan.

All too soon, the group came to a decision and
returned with the chief in the front.

"We have decided that the lives of many are more
important than the life of one," the chief said. He
sighed heavily as he looked at Rommy. "Little Walter
is younger than Alice is, and Hook is capable of great
evil. If you can avert a tragedy, then you must do it,
but there is no reason that you must die in doing so."

Rommy tried to swallow but the lump in her
throat made it difficult. It was an impossible choice.
She didn't want anyone to get hurt, but could she
purposely plot against her father - if this Hook even
was her father?

He turned to Pan. "Captain Hook will not trust
you have his daughter here since he has kept her a
secret all this time."

Pan looked at Rommy. "Do you have anything
that would show him I was telling the truth?"

"Before I do anything - what about Alice? I want her safe, no matter what happens to me." She turned to the chief. "I won't help anyone do anything if Alice isn't safe. I want your word because I know I can trust it."

A slight smile curved the chief's impassive face. "You must be like your mother in more than your looks, little one. You have courage." He nodded even as Tiger Lily snorted. "Yes, I give you my word that Alice will be safe."

"Will you get her home if she wants?" Rommy persisted.

Finn stepped forward. "I'll make sure she goes home if that's what she wants," he said.

Rommy ignored him and said to the chief, "Will you make sure he keeps his promise?"

She saw a flicker of hurt pass over Finn's face before his expression shuttered closed again.

The chief's voice was solemn. "Yes."

Rommy nodded once and then pulled her locket from inside her shirt. With trembling fingers she undid the latch. "Here," she said handing it to Pan. "My father gave this to me for tenth birthday. If Hook is my.. my father, he'll recognize this."

22
THE PLOT

Pan let out a triumphant laugh as his hand closed over the locket.

Alice held on to Rommy. "I won't leave you," she said. "I'm coming with you!"

"No, Alice," said Rommy. "You need to stay with Little Owl and the chief. They'll keep you safe. If you decide you want to go home, they'll get you there."

Alice tightened her arms around Rommy's waist and sniffled. "I don't want you to leave. I wish you really were my sister."

Rommy's lips trembled, and she hugged Alice back. "I do too, Alice." She wanted to promise the little girl that she'd be back and everything would be fine. Even at six, though, Alice had seen too much of life to fall for that lie. Rommy knew how it felt to have people give false reassurances that nobody really believed. She gently disengaged Alice's arms from around her waist.

Little Owl pulled Alice into her own arms. The little girl buried her face in the older woman's embrace. Rommy could hear her crying, and it broke her heart.

Chief Hawk Eye, Little Bear and Wolf walked Pan, Finn and Rommy to the edges of their encampment. The chief placed both hands on Rommy's shoulders. "May a blessing go with you, young one. Your sacrifice will not go unrewarded."

Rommy swallowed hard. Not sure what to say, she simply nodded and turned toward the boys.

"Come on," said Pan. He bounced from one foot to the other. "We have some Lost Boys to rescue." He gripped Rommy's arm and started to drag her along. She jerked away.

"I told you I'd come with you," she said. "There's no need to pull my arm out of the socket."

Pan sneered. "I don't know if I can trust Hook's daughter."

"Let her be, Pan," said Finn quietly.

"Taken in by her brave show?" Pan said.

"At least she's willing to put herself in jeopardy for the boys," said Finn under his breath.

Lightening quick, Pan was in Finn's face. "What did you say?"

Finn didn't back down but spoke louder. "I said

she's willing to help the boys, so we should get on with it."

"Don't forget who's the leader here." Pan narrowed his eyes, and a chill went up Rommy's spine. Despite still feeling hurt at Finn's betrayal, she didn't envy him if he crossed Pan. There was something vicious about Pan despite his young appearance.

The three of them moved away from the camp. Rommy purposefully did not look back. She didn't want to see Alice, or she might lose the little bit of courage she was clinging to.

Instead, she turned to Pan, determined to get more information out of him and distract him from Finn. Putting a touch of awe in her voice, she asked, "How long have you been the leader, Peter?"

"I've been here since before Hook and before Finn," said Pan. He threw back his shoulders. "Everyone knows I'm the leader." Pan shot a venomous look at Finn.

"How many Lost Boys do you take care of?" she pressed. She didn't know why but it seemed important to turn Pan's attention away from Finn. The tension between the two had thickened until it seemed to be a living thing.

"There are nine now since I found Walter," said Pan. "All of them follow me no matter where I go."

"I'm sure they must really admire you," said Rommy.

Pan beamed and flew in a quick circle before drawing next to her again. "You don't have to get hurt, Rommy. You just have to be the bait to help me get Hook. Once I've gotten rid of him, you can stay with us." He leaned in closer, peering into her face. "Can you really fight so well? Was Alice telling the truth?"

Rommy hesitated before speaking. She didn't liked to brag about herself, but even if she did, she wasn't sure how smart it was to tell Pan how well she could handle a sword. She shrugged. "You know Alice. She likes a good story. Those boys were so oafish, they were tripping over their own feet, and I would still have been a goner if Finn hadn't come when he did."

Pan pulled back and smiled. "I knew it! Girls aren't good fighters."

Rommy tried not to react, but the memory of Chattingham's fencing team made it hard not to laugh. She settled for a smile. "Are you a good fighter? You must be if you've escaped Captain Hook all this time."

She caught Finn's glance. He was watching her. When she caught his eye, he gave the barest nod of his head. He knew what she was doing, and he approved. Rommy wasn't sure what to make of him. On the one hand, he had betrayed her and Alice, but she got the sense he didn't really like Pan all that much, either.

Pan didn't seem to notice or care how Finn felt. He was too busy telling Rommy about what a great sword fighter he was. He pulled a dirk from a sheath by his side to show her a few of his moves. Not as long as a sword, its blade was still almost a foot long making it dangerous. Its biggest drawback was that you had to get fairly close to your opponent to strike, and it was heavy.

"This time, I'll get Hook," Pan finished, putting his dirk back in its sheath with a flourish.

Rommy knew she had to tread carefully. "How will you do that? I thought you wanted to rescue the Lost Boys. How can you rescue them and get Captain Hook?"

"You think I can't do it, don't you? Well, I'll tell you so you can see how smart I am—too smart for Hook and too smart for his daughter!"

Rommy cocked her head. She didn't have to try to appear interested.

"I'll bait the hook for Hook." He cackled at his own joke. "You'll draw Hook away, so he's off his ship. Without the ship's magic, he can't fly at all. Once I get Hook to let the Lost Boys go and leave his ship to save you, I'll take care of him. Then we'll go back and take over the ship." He hooted with laughter again, slapping his knees. "It won't be the Lost Boys and Pan who will walk the plank!"

Rommy wrinkled her nose. "I don't understand. Why can't Hook fly? I can still fly here."

Finn answered this time. "Grown-ups can't believe enough to fly without a constant dusting of pixie dust, and even then, it's only some of them. Neverland has magic children can tap into it without trying much. You need pixie dust and belief to get here, but once you're here," he shrugged, "I guess that's enough."

Rommy looked up at Pan who was now flying in loops over their heads. "I still don't quite understand the plan. How will you get Captain Hook to let the Lost Boys go and come after me?"

Pan landed beside her. His smile was cold. "You'll see. It's quite clever." He zipped up into the sky again.

23

THE REVENGE

As the three of them made their way along the river, the sun rose and got warmer. Rommy had no idea what time it was, but looking at the sky, she thought it must be late morning by now.

They passed the willow tree where she and Alice had found shelter. She bit her lip. She hoped Alice would be all right whatever happened.

Finn seemed to read her mind. He leaned toward her and whispered, "Little Owl and the chief will take good care of Alice. You don't have to worry, and I'll bring her back to London if she wants."

Rommy gave him a hard stare. "I trust them to keep *their* word. Thankfully, I don't have to count on you."

Finn's face fell, but he said nothing else.

Rommy and Finn continued to walk in the long grass by the river while Pan flew above them, taking frequent detours and then zipping back to hurry them along.

The last thing Rommy wanted to do was hurry. She didn't know what Pan planned for her, but the longer she could stall him, the more time she had to figure a way out of this mess.

As they rounded a curve in the river, Rommy recognized the patch of tall reeds where the monster reptile had almost snapped her and Alice up for his dinner. She shuddered and tried to put some distance between herself and the riverbank.

"What's the matter? Afraid of old Crocky?" said Pan, flying up beside her.

"Crocky?" Rommy asked.

Instead of answering, Pan sped toward the river and skimmed along the surface. He alighted on a floating log and lightly ran down its length.

The log erupted out of the water, and Pan used the creature's long snout as a ramp. He pushed off the animal's nose and flew out of its reach as it snapped its jaws on empty air.

Rommy shoved into the air and hovered above the ground. "What is that thing?" she asked as Pan came tumbling beside her, laughing so hard he was bent almost double.

"It's a crocodile." Pan pointed to the creature who had settled back to floating in the water, but its yellow eyes still watched them. "He's the reason your dear old dad only has one hand."

Rommy stared after Pan as he buzzed forward, and then flew to catch up to him. Finn joined them in the air, and they continued on.

It seemed to take a much shorter time to arrive back at the caves than it had leaving them last night.

Pan pointed imperiously to a rock outside the cave. "Sit there and wait."

Rommy walked over to the rock and perched on its edge. Once he saw she had obeyed his order, Pan flew into the cave opening. It didn't take him long to reappear with two long vines.

"Come on," he said. He flitted by both Finn and Rommy and headed up the sides of the rock wall. Rommy and Finn followed him. Rommy could feel the mist as it sprayed off the waterfall in a rainbow of colors.

As they topped the cliff edge, the jungle came into view. Rommy hoped Pan wasn't planning on stashing her somewhere in there. Who knew what dreadful creatures it contained.

Pan flew beside her. "Don't get any ideas about trying to escape," he said. "I'll go back for Alice if you do. Besides, if you help me, you won't have to die." He laughed and sped up.

Rommy didn't find Pan's words very reassuring. His moods changed as often as the wind shifted. She remembered how he had laughed when the flower had eaten the bird and shivered. He might find it funny to watch her die. As Alice had said, he was balmy in the crumpet.

Finn, who had lagged behind the other two, now drew even with Rommy. "I... I don't want you to get hurt," he said in a low voice.

"You have a funny way of showing it," Rommy said, her voice hard.

"Look, Hook isn't above hurting the Lost Boys. He'll do anything to get Pan. Some of those boys are younger than Alice. Pan won't give himself up to help them. He doesn't really care. If they die, he'll just take more."

"What do you mean, take more? I thought Lost Boys were just that—lost—like Alice."

"Never mind that," said Finn. "The point is, I have to help them. I'd give myself up, but Hook only wants Pan. That's all he's ever wanted since he got here." Finn shook his head. "Look, I just wanted you to know I'll try to help you if I can."

"Trying to make up with her," said Pan who had a habit of springing up out of nowhere. Pan looked at Rommy's face and punched Finn's shoulder. "That's not going to happen anytime soon."

Finn's face turned pink and he put on speed, pulling away from them. Rommy looked at Pan. "Where are we going? Somewhere in the jungle?"

"Nope! My plan is genius. It's a kind of poetic justice for old Hook." He giggled.

It didn't take long for them to reach the end of the

jungle and arrive at the pink sand beach where Rommy and Alice had first touched down in Neverland.

Rommy's stomach flipped as she looked at the turquoise waters below them. She hoped Pan wasn't going to throw her to the mermaids. The idea of those beautiful creatures pulling her beneath the water made her mouth go dry with fear.

Pan swooped onto the beach. Finn and Rommy followed at a slower pace.

Once they all stood together, Pan pointed to the large rock in the middle of the lagoon. The water barely lapped at the edges of the formation, but even from here Rommy could see that when the tide came in, the rock would be completely submerged except for the topmost point. She had a sick feeling she knew what Pan was planning.

Pan cackled and clapped his hands. "It's perfect. Captain Hook tied up Tiger Lily and put her on that rock until she told him where my hideout was. Bless her, she wouldn't say a word, and she almost drowned. Now, I'm going to put you in the same place." He went off on another peal of laughter.

Rommy's stomach went liquid and her legs got wobbly.

Pan tossed a vine to Finn. "Tie her up."

Rommy backed up a step. If she was quick, she could fly away. They'd probably catch her, but she'd buy more time.

Pan grabbed her arm and pushed his face close to hers. "Remember little Alice. If you think I can't get to her, you're wrong. Tiger Lily will do anything for me."

Rommy's lips quivered, and she pushed them together. She wouldn't give Pan the satisfaction.

"So brave," he cooed at her. "Maybe I won't let you drown. I rather like you, even if you are Hook's daughter." He turned to Finn. "What are you waiting for? An invitation from the queen? Tie her up! We have work to do."

Finn looked apologetic as he wrapped the vines around her wrist and then wound them around her torso. As he moved behind her, he whispered into her ear, "I won't let you drown. I promise."

Rommy didn't feel very reassured by this promise since he had lied to her and brought her here to begin with. She had no doubt that the Lost Boys were his first priority. Not her.

The two boys hefted her between them and flew out to the rock and set her down. "May as well sit down and get comfortable, pirate princess," said Pan. "The tide won't be in until almost sunset."

Rommy sat cross-legged on the flattest surface of the rock where it met a piece that jutted into the sky. She pushed her back against it, and Pan threw the other vine to Finn. "Tie her to the rock. We don't want her getting away now, do we?"

The rope tugged Rommy more tightly against the back of the rock, but it wasn't uncomfortable.

Pan came to crouch by her side. "Maybe, I'll even let you say goodbye to your papa before I rid Neverland of him once and for all." He patted her cheek and then nodded at Finn.

The two of them leapt off the rock into the sky.

24
THE MERMAID

Rommy leaned her head back against the rock and watched until Finn and Pan were mere specks in the sky and then gone all together. The light breeze tugged at her hair, tangling it around her face. The sun made diamonds on the dancing water.

She could see fish swimming in the clear blue waters lapping against the base of the rock where she was tied. Sea birds wheeled in the sky, occasionally diving toward the surface of the water. From here, she saw the edge of the jungle on the tops of the cliffs. Birds flitted in and out of the foliage that tangled up its sides.

It would have been peaceful if she wasn't tied to a rock waiting to drown.

Since she had left Chattingham's yesterday, she had been running from one disaster to another. Was it only yesterday?

Rommy thought back. Yes, it was yesterday she had left the school because she had started this morning in the camp with Chief Hawk Eye, Little Owl and the rest. That seemed ages ago. Chattingham's and Francie were a lifetime ago.

Rommy briefly wondered how Francie was doing. Surely, her disappearance had been discovered by now. She hoped Francie wouldn't get in too much trouble.

A bird wheeled near the rock and came to sit on one of its outcroppings. It cocked its head at her. "All I wanted to do was find Papa," she said to the bird. It jutted its bright pink head forward and stared at her with its small eyes as if it was listening. "I just wanted some information. I didn't plan on coming to this magical island and getting involved in I don't know what." She sighed. "Do you think this Captain Hook is my papa?" The bird made a chirping noise and lifted back into the air.

Rommy closed her eyes. She desperately wished Francie was here. Poor Francie would feel so guilty if she disappeared. She'd likely think Rommy fell afoul of footpads. Rommy gave a small, watery laugh. Francie would never guess what really happened, that was for sure.

With another sigh, Rommy pulled her hands up as far as possible and leaned down. She could just reach the vines with her mouth. She pulled with her teeth as hard as she could. The vines weren't too tight. Finn had left them a bit loose, but from her position, she couldn't get enough leverage to get them to move much.

She stopped pulling. Could she chew through them? She took a tentative bite, but their outsides were smooth and hard. She couldn't even get her teeth to puncture the surface.

Rommy looked around as far as her position allowed. There had to be something. She wasn't going to sit here on this rock and wait to drown. If she could get loose from the rope that bound her to the rock, she might be able to rub the vines around her wrists on the rough surface enough to cut through them.

She craned her neck up and noticed that the part of rock they tied her to became skinnier the higher it went. If she could only stand up, the rope would loosen and she could slide out.

Rommy pulled her feet under her as far as she could and pushed up. She only managed to move a couple inches before she plopped back down with a groan.

With grim determination, Rommy pulled her feet in again even tighter this time. She leaned against the rock as hard as she could and pushed with her feet. This time she moved almost a foot before her feet slipped on the algae-covered surface.

"Oh look, Arista," a musical voice called out. "It looks like someone left us a lovely little plaything."

Rommy looked around and spotted a sleek black head. A blonde head popped up next to it. Great, she muttered under her breath. Just what she needed — murderous mermaids. As if things weren't difficult enough.

The blonde had flipped on her back and was using her tail to send waves of water over the base of the rock. The water wasn't quite high enough to wash over where Rommy was sitting, but in a few hours it probably would be.

Not happy with the waves, the blonde brought her tail down hard on the water's surface of the water and sent a wet spray over Rommy.

"Maybe we should let her go, Adella," Arista called to her sister. "It might be fun to discover what happens."

A red head popped up a distance away. "Yes, let's, Adella," the redhead said. Her eyes were on Rommy, but unlike the cold green of Adella's eyes, there was kindness in her golden gaze.

"I don't know, Adrina," said Adella. She did a lazy circle around the rock. She looked up at Rommy who had been silent during the entire exchange. "Why are you tied to this rock?"

Rommy wasn't sure if she should tell anything to this creature who had no love of humans, but it wasn't as if she had many options. Maybe the mermaid would let her go just to cause trouble. She seemed to like doing that.

"I'm to be the bait on the hook to catch a bigger Hook," she said.

The blonde let out a silvery laugh. "Why would Captain Hook come to save you? Pan has some silly ideas!"

A smile curved Adella red lips. "There must be more to it. Who is Captain Hook to you?"

Rommy said nothing. She didn't think she wanted this mermaid to know Hook might be her father.

"You must be someone he cares about if Pan thinks he'll come to save you." She continued to swim lazily around the rock. It reminded Rommy of the stories of sharks circling shipwrecks. She shuddered. The mermaid halted. "Why would Captain Hook want to save you, girl child?"

Rommy remained silent. Arista and Adella resumed circling the rock. The redheaded one had disappeared. She wished they'd all go away.

Adella stopped again. "We'll be back. After all, you aren't going anywhere." Her laugh made Rommy wince.

Arista surfaced and slapped her tail again, drenching Rommy. She shook her wet hair out of her face.

Both mermaids gave a flick of their tails and sped away, leaving a v-shaped wave in their wake.

Rommy gathered her feet under her again and pushed again. This time though, the vines gave way.

She fell forward, barely catching herself before she fell on her face.

On her hands and knees she looked around trying to figure out what had just happened. Had Adella cut the rope? Or maybe it was the blonde one. She seemed to like playing tricks.

Whichever one had done it, Rommy didn't care. She needed to get these vines off her hands and come up with some kind of plan. As she pushed herself to a standing position, an object plunked down at her feet. Bending over, she realized it was a shell, a razor sharp one.

It seemed too good to be true that one of the mermaids had given her something to cut her bonds. Then she spotted a red head surfacing near the rock base. The mermaid met her gaze and smiled shyly at Rommy. Then, with a flick of her tail, she disappeared.

"Wait," Rommy called, wanting to thank her.

But the mermaid had simply vanished.

Rommy didn't know why this mermaid seemed different from her sisters, but whatever the reason, she wasn't about to let the gift of her freedom go to waste. Although it was difficult, she managed to saw at the vines until they finally broke apart. She tucked the shell into her pocket. It might come in handy. Now all she had to do was get to Captain Hook's ship in time.

25

THE FLIGHT

Now that she was free, Rommy felt frozen with indecision. Pan and Finn had both mentioned the Cove when referring to Captain Hook, but where was that? When she and Alice had tried to escape, the river seemed like the obvious way to find the Cove, but what if she was wrong? She didn't know how big Neverland was, and every moment of indecision that ticked by felt urgently important.

Flying off the rock, Rommy hovered high enough so she could see that the lagoon led to the open sea around the island. One possibility was to follow the coastline. Surely, the Cove would be obvious from there, but if Hook had left his boat, wouldn't he have to come by land? Pan said he wouldn't be able to fly. It seemed more risky to go along the river, more likely she'd run into someone she didn't want to see her. Rommy groaned with frustration. Why did everything come down to directions when she was absolutely horrible at them?

Decide, she told herself. Taking a breath, she headed toward the sea and flew along the rocky coast, staying low. Straying over the white-capped waves of the surrounding sea, she faltered, losing altitude. For a moment, panic swamped her as the waves rose up to meet her. Desperately, she put on a burst of speed and headed inland. If the mermaids were dangerous, who knew what else lurked in these waters. Rommy had no wish to find out.

As she got closer to the rocks that marked the edges of the island, she once again found herself flying without effort. The magic of Neverland must have a boundary line. She'd have to be careful not to cross it again.

The coast was rugged with imposing rocks that dotted the waters around the island. Anyone trying to land a boat here would find it difficult.

She paused at several inlets, but they were too small for a ship to pass through. After the third one, Rommy began to wonder how far the Cove was from the lagoon. Urgency pushed at her.

The fifth inlet led to a rollicking stretch of water wide enough for a ship. Rommy followed it and found it dumped into a large, sheltered bay. Pausing at an outcropping of rocks, she heard him before she saw him. It was Pan's crowing laughter that carried on the breeze. Rommy touched down behind the rocks and crouched. Carefully, she peered around the edge.

The Cove was surrounded almost completely by a rocky beach that gradually climbed up into more cliffs on two sides. Rommy saw an opening between them where a more placid river flowed. That must have been the river she had been following earlier.

Anchored just off the rocky beach in front of the farthest cliff, a large ship floated. From here, she could make out people moving around on its deck. A large man was standing at the bow. He appeared to be shaking what she guessed was his fist. When the sun caught it, Rommy realized it was a hook. A shiny silver hook. Identical to the one her father sported on his left arm.

Pan was hovering just out of reach off the bow, laughing. His back was to her.

When the big man moved forward, Rommy saw two bodies, one much taller than the other. They appeared to be tied to one of the masts. They were too far away to identify, but a faint light flickering near the taller one's head made Rommy's stomach sink with the realization it was probably Finn.

She heard Pan's high, clear voice call out, "Time's a'wasting, Captain. High tide is coming, and you'll have to find your daughter in order to save her!" He laughed again.

"You better hope I do, Pan," the big man

bellowed, "unless you want to lose your second in command and the youngest member of your little band of brats."

"I can always find more Lost Boys. Can you find another daughter?" Pan taunted.

On the far shore where the other river entered the Cove, a group of children were cheering and whooping every time Pan spoke. Those must be the Lost Boys, Rommy thought.

Pan was right. Time was a 'wasting. It looked like the Lost Boys were safe and the captain hadn't left his boat just yet. She had made it in time.

Now to get on deck without Pan seeing her or giving herself away. Taking a deep breath, Rommy crept out from behind her hiding spot and flew over the channel of water that marked the entrance to the Cove. She alighted on the opposite side and made her way toward the ship. Trying to stay hidden, Rommy didn't dare fly. She picked her way along the craggy banks, silently giving thanks for the jagged rocks that kept her hidden from view.

Even though she was moving as quickly as she could, Rommy still felt the relentless passing of time. She had to reach the ship before the captain left. She still couldn't give him the name Papa, even in her thoughts.

Finally, she was even with the boat. Creeping out from a large boulder, she flew across the water, so close to its surface that small waves splashed the front of her shirt. Following the hull of the boat, Rommy drew even with the deck rail, slipped over, and touched down. A large cabin situated toward the stern of the boat hid her arrival. Rommy hugged the sides of the cabin as she glided toward the main deck where everyone had gathered. If Pan had been paying better attention, he would have seen her skulking around the side of the cabin. But he was too busy taunting the captain and bragging about himself. Rommy rolled her eyes. Typical.

The waves lapping the boat and the creaking of the mast and sails overhead made it harder to hear everything being said out on the main deck. Rommy paused at the corner of the cabin. Open deck stretched out before her, and she could see the men. They stood frozen like a strange museum exhibit.

From here Pan's face was visible. He still hadn't spotted her, he was so focused on the pirate in front of him. Rommy studied the back of the man Pan was taunting.

He wore a long leather coat of oxblood red. His long black hair flowed over his shoulders.

"If you've harmed a hair on her head, I will roast you on a spit," a familiar voice said.

Rommy's breath caught in her throat, and she stared at the back of the big man. When the captain turned, the two bodies tied to the mast came into view. She had been right. One of them was Finn. The other was a small, blond-headed boy. He was crying and Finn was talking to him although she couldn't make out the words. Everyone else's eyes remained riveted on their captain and Pan. Nobody noticed as Rommy slowly walked out from the shadow of the cabin.

As she padded closer, the captain put the tip of his sharp hook delicately under the little boy's chin and lifted it. Then he leaned down. The little boy pulled back as far as his bonds let him. Tears flowed down his cheeks, and even from here, Rommy saw his whole body quivering. She doubted he'd still be standing if the ropes hadn't held him to the mast.

Finn said something, but the words were lost in the wind blowing through the forest of masts and rigging. The man turned to stare at the taller boy, his face twisting into a snarling mask. The hook whipped out, landing with an audible thunk a hair's breadth from the side of Finn's face.

Rommy flinched and darted forward, pushing through the startled men. "No, Papa!"

The man froze mid-snarl and then turned to look at her. His blue eyes burned into her, pinning her to the deck. Rommy had to make herself not take a step back.

Slowly the man pulled his hook from the wooden mast. An ugly gouge remained. Straightening to his full height, the man stepped forward. "Andromeda? So, you really are here. I didn't want to believe it."

Rommy lifted her chin, never breaking eye contact with her father. "There are a lot of things I didn't want to believe either, Papa," she said in a quiet voice.

26

THE PIRATE

"No, no, no, no!!" The shriek brought Hook and Rommy up short. For a moment, they had both forgotten Pan who now pointed at Rommy accusingly. "How did you get out? Why did you ruin my plan? I was so close!"

Spinning in the air, he took off toward the group of boys on the shore. He looked over his shoulder. The snarl on his face was frightening in its intensity. "You'll pay for this, Rommy. You're no better than your father!"

Rommy stared at the retreating figure of Pan. She couldn't help the shiver that traveled up her spine. Pan was frightening even when he wasn't her enemy.

"Andromeda!" Her father's voice was always booming. He took two large strides, and before she knew what was happening, he had scooped her up in his arms and off her feet. "Andromeda." This time he murmured her name against her hair.

For a moment, Rommy closed her eyes and let her father hold her. For the first time since climbing into that milk wagon forever ago, she was safe. Her papa was here, and he was alive.

With a final kiss on her head, Hook set her on her feet before giving her a gentle shake. "What were you thinking, young lady? Why are you here and not in Chattingham's where I left you safe and sound? You have some explaining to do."

Rommy stared up at her father. His hair which he usually kept contained in a neat queue, flowed around his shoulders. There were gold buttons on his coat, and a small gold hoop winked in his ear. He looked familiar, yet different. Perhaps it was the black flag with a skull and cross bones that flew far above his head.

Which reminded her. Finn and the little boy were still tied to the mast. There were so many things she needed to say, to ask, but her attention was caught on the two boys. The younger boy's head hung and she could hear him sniffling. She saw Finn's mouth move. He was looking at the little boy. After a moment, the child lifted his head, and Rommy saw a small, watery smile curve his lips.

She looked around the deck. There were about a

dozen men, all strangers. They were frozen in various activities. All of them were staring at her. A few of them had their mouths hanging open. She was suddenly aware of her hair straggling around her face, the rip down her sleeve, and her dirty, crumpled clothing.

"Well? Do you have anything to say for yourself, Andromeda?" Hook's voice was stern, and his brows were pulled low over his eyes. The tenderness of a moment ago had vanished.

Rommy remembered all she had been through to get here: the worry, the fear, the near death experience. Then there were the lies. So many lies. Something in her snapped.

Rommy gestured around the deck. "You're the one who has some explaining to do, Papa. I'm not the one who has a secret life. I'm not the one who spends all of his time as a pirate on a magic island fighting children! Children, Papa? I'm not the one who lied over and over." With each word, Rommy's voice had climbed until she was shouting. "You want an explanation? I was worried about you. I was afraid something horrible had happened to you when you didn't show up for my birthday. So I went to your offices to see if I could find something out, but there was nothing there but dust. Lots and lots of dust. Years of dust." Her voice broke on the last word.

"Andromeda..." Hook started, but a small, round man came bustling forward.

"Now, Andromeda, dear, Captain Hook will explain things to you, but you must be exhausted."

"Mr. Smee?" Rommy asked, incredulous. "But, I thought… that is to say… I mean, aren't you a bookkeeper?"

"Oh dear me, just call me Smee," the small man said pulling at the white fringe of hair that ran around his shiny, bald head. "Well, not exactly. I mean, yes, I have always helped the Captain where and when he needs it. And he needs me here." Smee put a gentle hand under Rommy's elbow and started to lead her toward a short flight of stairs.

Twisting out of his grasp, Rommy said, "I still haven't gotten any answers."

"No, you haven't," agreed Smee, taking hold of her arm again. "But you will, my dear, just you wait." He towed her along.

Rommy tried to plant her feet, but Smee just kept moving her forward somehow, talking all the while.

"Let's get your settled in the Captain's quarters, maybe get you a little dinner, and then you and your father can have a nice chat." He patted her arm and noticed the cuts on her hands. "Yes, and we'll get those all fixed up too."

Rommy found herself at the top of a short set of stairs that led to the cabin that apparently belonged to her father. As Smee ushered her into her father's quarters she swiveled around to look back. Her father was standing in the middle of the deck staring after her. His scowl was the last thing she saw before the door closed behind her.

Her father's quarters were spacious. A screen separated what appeared to be a sleeping area from a large table that was nailed to the floor and surrounded by heavy, curved chairs. Maps, compasses and other navigating equipment littered its surface. A big chest sat against one wall. Next to it was a pot-bellied stove.

Smee pushed her into the chair closest to the stove and then bustled over to it. Rommy tried to stand back up, but Smee simply pushed her back down, gently but insistently. It didn't take long before a merry little fire was burning in the stove's belly sending warmth into the room. A tea kettle sat on top, steam rising from its spout. Rommy watched Mr. Smee—she could think of him as nothing else—as he went around the screen. He reappeared a moment later with a blanket and a small black bag under his arm. He tucked the blanket around her and pulled a small footstool under her feet. She tried to push it off, but he tucked it back again, undeterred.

He pulled up another stool and took her hands, turning them this way and that. Then he pulled out small pots of ointment from his bag and smeared the ointment on the cuts on her hands. She must have done it while she was cutting those vines, but she hadn't even noticed. He expertly wound bandages around each hand and placed her hands back in her lap. The tea kettle whistled, and he bounced up. He turned his back to her as he fussed with her tea before he brought it to her.

"There now, you just drink that up. It'll make you feel better," he said. "I'll be right back with a bite of dinner. Your father should be right along to join you. He has to get those scalawags on deck back to their jobs." He chuckled. "Any excuse to loaf." The small man bustled right out the door, still chattering away leaving Rommy feeling like she had just experienced a small, kind-hearted tornado.

She shook her head, slightly bewildered, and sipped the tea. It had a strange, bitter taste, but her thoughts were in such a muddle, she hardly noticed. She couldn't quite believe she was here and she had found her father. And he was a pirate.

She was glad—so glad—he was safe.

But, he had lied to her. For years. For her entire life really. That man on deck was not the father she knew. In so many ways, he was a stranger. The burning anger she had felt on deck flickered, but a wave of drowsiness doused it.

Too late, she realized the unrelenting sleepiness that was dragging her under wasn't quite right. Her eyelids drooped and even though she fought it, she couldn't keep them open. Rommy knew she needed her father to explain things. She needed to know why he had lied to her all these years. But the gentle rocking of the boat and the warmth of the fire and that irresistible drowsiness pulled her under. Her last thought was that she needed to help Finn and that little boy.

27
THE REALITY

When Rommy opened her eyes, she was no longer sitting in the chair by the little pot-bellied stove. Instead, she was lying in a soft bed, her head cradled by a fluffy pillow. A dim, watery light was coming through the window on the other side of the screen.

Was it morning? By her best guess, it had been mid-afternoon when she had arrived here yesterday. Had she been asleep this entire time? Her head felt heavy and messy, like it was filled with cobwebs. She shook it to clear her thoughts, and then she remembered the bitter tea and the unusual sleepiness. She pushed herself up and climbed out of the bed. Her feet were bare. Her father, or maybe Mr. Smee, had removed her boots.

She padded around the screen, but the room was

empty. She was wondering if she should go out to find someone when there was a knock at the door.

"Um, come in?" Rommy said.

Smee poked his head in. "You're up at last! You slept the day and night away." He came in carrying a tray of breakfast. "Poor lamb. You were plumb exhausted." He set the tray on the table.

Rommy crossed her arms and looked at him. "I don't recollect being quite that exhausted," she said.

"Oh my, whatever do you mean?" Smee continued to bustle around the room.

"What I mean is I think you put something in my tea to help me sleep so long, Mr. Smee."

"Just Smee, dear. In your tea, you say? Oh dear me, nothing so sinister as all that. I only added a little valerian and lemon balm. They're completely harmless and help to relax you. You wouldn't have slept this long if you didn't need it, dear."

Rommy continued to eye him suspiciously, but she had to admit she felt better than she had since this whole adventure had started. Smee steered her toward a chair by the table. "Why don't you sit right here and eat up. I bet you're absolutely starved." He took the bundle he was carrying and laid them over the back of a chair. "I brought you some fresh clothes. They might be a little big, but they're clean. I'll have Stubbs and Tommy bring in hot water so you can get cleaned up." He paused and his face turned pink. "And, well, if you need to take care of any, well, *busi-*

ness, the chamber pot is over in the far corner. Tommy will empty it later."

Rommy's face turned warm, and she thought it was probably pinker than Mr. Smee's. "Thank you. You don't have to go to all this trouble for me."

"Oh, dear, of course I do," he said. "You're a pirate princess now."

Rommy simply stared at him.

"Eat up, now. By the time you're done, the boys will have that hot water ready and tote it in here for you."

"Where is Papa?"

"I'll take you out to see him when you're done eating, and all cleaned up. You'll feel so much better." Smee beamed at her and then turned to go.

"Wait," said Rommy as a horrible thought hit her. "Those boys, the ones tied to the mast, they aren't still there are they?"

Smee chuckled. "Oh, aren't you so sweet? Don't worry your pretty little head about those boys. They're perfectly fine."

Rommy stepped in front of Smee to stop him from leaving. "I'm serious. I want to know if they're all right. Won't Papa let them go now? Why would he want to keep them?"

Smee patted her cheek affectionately. "Don't you worry about those boys. I'm sure your dear papa will return them very soon."

"But…"

"But nothing," said Smee moving Rommy out of the way. "You eat your breakfast, and I'll go get that water started for you. You don't want to keep the captain waiting too long, do you?" Smee was out the door before Rommy could say anything at all.

She put her hand on the door knob to follow, but it refused to turn. Before she could work up any indignation that he had locked her in, her stomach gave a loud growl. Better eat so she could face Papa at full strength. If someone had asked her even three days ago if she could convince her father to let a couple boys go, she would have said yes. Now, she wasn't so sure. Of course, three days ago, there would have been no reason whatsoever for Papa to tie two boys to a ship mast.

Rommy sat down and ate. The eggs were fluffy, the bacon was crisp, and the fruit was delicious, even though it wasn't anything she could identify. She had barely scraped the last food onto her fork when there was another knock on the door.

"Yes?" she called.

A gruff voice said, "Beggin' your pardon, miss, but I've gots yer water."

"Come in," she said.

After a moment of rattling, the door flew open and she bit back a gasp. A grizzled old man stood there. He had a patch over one eye, and one of his legs ended in a wooden stump.

"Come on, Stubbs," said a much younger voice.

"This tub's heavy. Get yer backside moving afore I drop it all over the deck. Then Captain'll be hot under the collar."

The older man smiled at her. She tried not to stare at the gaping holes where teeth should have been. Instead, she tentatively smiled back. "Um, Mr. Stubbs is it?"

The older man laughed, shaking his half of the tub. Water sloshed over the sides. He didn't seem to notice. "Mr. Stubbs. How do ya like that, boy? A fine lady is the Captain's daughter. Where would ya like yer tub, Miss Andromeda?"

Rommy looked around the room. "Oh, here in front of the stove is just fine," she said.

Stubbs came in with the front half of the tub. A freckled-faced boy with a mop of rich chestnut hair brought up the other half. He nodded his head at her. "Morning, miss," he said.

"Hello," Rommy said, smiling at him. "Thank you both very much for the water."

The boy beamed at her, and the older man did a sort of half bow. "Such genteel manners," he mumbled as the two of them made their way out the door. "Now, that's a little lady if I ever did see one."

She heard the boy laugh. "When's the last time you seen a lady, Stubbs?"

Stubbs growled something, but the door shut cutting off his words. The port hole window was far enough away that nobody could see in even if they dared to look. Somehow with the way the men referred to her father, she guessed nobody would. Still, she felt a bit shy getting undressed in this strange place. That shyness evaporated though when she sank into the hot water. She gave a sigh of bliss. She felt like she was carrying the grime of a thousand years on her.

Rommy spent a few minutes soaking, but then got to work cleaning herself. She even washed her hair, dunking her entire head to rinse it off. When she got out and toweled off, a sense of optimism buoyed her spirits.

Mr. Smee had been right after all, she reflected, as she pulled on the clean clothes. She was afraid of what she'd find once she left this cabin, but being clean and having a full stomach helped her feel more ready to face it. She carefully rolled up the pant legs and the sleeves which were both too long. Taking the belt off her trousers, she fastened it around her waist. Next, she rolled on the socks and pulled on her boots. After using one of her father's combs to brush the knots out of her wet hair, she braided it. She almost felt like her old self.

Sadness replaced some of her optimism. The truth was, she could never go back to her old self. Her old self had no idea about all of this. She had thought Papa was a noble man, not a pirate. She'd believed Papa never lied to her. Rommy's shoulders drooped. For a moment, she desperately wished she could go back to three days ago and not know any of this. Her life hadn't been perfect, but this, she didn't know what to do with this.

After a moment, Rommy shook those thoughts away and squared her shoulders. The reality was, her old life was a lie. All those things she thought were true, weren't. She might not have known about this secret life her father led, but that didn't change that it was a reality. While it would be easier not to know all of this, Rommy decided she'd rather know the truth than only think she did.

With this thought fresh in her mind, she put her hand on the door knob. Stubbs had forgotten to lock it again. After a slight hesitation, she pulled the door open and stepped out on the deck. It was time to talk to her father.

28
THE FIGHT

When Rommy walked out onto the deck, she spotted a giant of a man with a flaming red beard that fell to his waist. He was whistling cheerfully as he wrapped thick ropes into a coil and dropped them back onto the deck. Then the man cupped his hand around his mouth and bellowed up into a tangle of rigging high above their heads, "Max, did you check the top sail?"

Rommy looked up into the forest of rigging and a sun-streaked head popped up. "Aye, Red, all looks shipshape up here," the voice called. Nimble as any monkey, the young man climbed down from the top rigging and was standing on the deck so fast, Rommy blinked at him. He looked older than her or Finn, but he wasn't quite a man either. The boy caught her staring at him and gave her a quick grin. He started toward her, but the giant laid a beefy hand on his shoulder. "I'd steer clear, lad. That's the captain's daughter, and we have work to do. You need to get up the foremast and check the sail up there. Hop to it!"

"I was just going to say hello, Red," the young man complained. "Twern't like was going to propose."

The giant named Red clapped him on the back and the boy staggered several steps. "See that you aren't too friendly, boy. I don't think the captain would like it." The bearded man smiled and nodded at Rommy. She returned the smile. It was hard not to.

Max looked at Rommy and winked. Then he shrugged and sauntered to one of the lesser masts and scrambled back up into the rigging.

Rommy was still staring up after him when Smee came bustling up. "Ah, there you are, all clean and fed." He frowned. "You should have waited for me in the cabin."

"Good morning, Mr. Smee. I'd like to see my father now, if you please."

"Oh, dear me, now isn't a good time, my darling girl." Smee took hold of her elbow and tried to steer her back toward the captain's quarters. Instead of letting herself be led away, Rommy pulled her arm away from the round, little man.

"I won't be put off again," she said and strode toward the opposite end of the boat. She could hear

Smee huffing and puffing behind her. "But Miss Andromeda, wait," he called as she put on more speed, lengthening the distance between them.

The deck was clear even though the sun had risen. She did see a burly man over by the anchor, his bald head shining in the morning sun. She wasn't sure what he was doing, but his scowl drew attention to an ugly scar that ran down one side of his face. He glanced up and caught her looking at him. Unlike the others she had encountered, he didn't smile at her. Instead his lip curled in annoyance and after a brief glare, he went back to what he had been doing.

His expression gave her a jolt, and she thought she wouldn't want to be on his bad side. Hurrying, she fought the urge to glance behind her to see if he was watching her.

She reached the steps leading to the bow. She could see her father standing at the wheel of the ship. Finn and the little boy were still tied up, but they had been allowed to sit down at least. Rommy sucked in a breath of outrage, but before she could speak, the captain turned.

Noticing her, his brows came down in annoyance. Then with an effort, he cleared his expression and arranged his face into a smile.

"Andromeda, darling, what are you doing out here? I thought I told Smee to have you wait in my quarters. I have a few small things to take care of yet." He nodded to the two boys.

"Yes, about them, why haven't you freed them yet?" she demanded. "That poor little boy is terrified."

"Look here, young lady, you understand nothing of how this ship or this island works." The smile Hook had arranged on his face slid off replaced by a ferocious frown. "You need to get back to my quarters. Now."

Smee came to a stop behind her, out of breath. "That's what I was telling her, Captain," he said. "I'll just take her back now, or maybe she wants a bit of fresh air. We can take a turn around the deck. I can introduce you to a few of the fellows and.."

"Absolutely not!" bellowed Hook. "I will not have Andromeda being friendly with my crew. Where is your brain, Smee? Take her back to my cabin."

Hook turned away, clearly dismissing her. Rommy felt the anger that had flickered last night roar up. She wouldn't be surprised if steam started coming out of her ears.

"I will not go back to the cabin," she said. "Not until you answer my questions and not until you let those boys go. Why if you only knew…" Behind her father, Finn's eyes got big and he was shaking his head at her… "…if you only knew how awful it was to be tied up and helpless, you'd know how wicked this is, Papa."

Hook spun back toward her, his expression glowering. "Don't make me repeat myself, Andromeda. This is none of your concern."

Rommy took a step forward, the toes of her boots almost touching his. "Not my concern? Not my concern? I came all the way from London to find you, to see if you were all right. You forgot all about me because you were too busy fighting children. You've been lying practically all my life and this is none of my concern? Instead of answers all you tell me to do is go sit in your cabin. I won't do it!" Her voice had risen until once again she was shouting at her father. She felt as much as heard the bustle on the deck go still. The crew held their breath to see what their captain would do.

Her father's blue eyes snapped with anger and he leaned forward, his voice coming out in a hiss. "You will keep your voice down and do what I say, Andromeda. Do not defy me, not here."

Angry tears pricked at Rommy's eyes, but seeing the men staring at them, she lowered her voice. "Defy you? I just want to understand why you are doing this. What made you leave me and our life together to do this, to be a pirate of all things? I don't understand."

Hook's face softened, and he put his hands on her shoulders. "I know you don't. I will try to explain things, I promise, but you must trust me and go back to the cabin now."

Rommy shrugged off his hands, her expression

hardening again. "That's the thing, I can't trust you anymore, not when you've lied to me for years. Not when you have two boys tied up. Are you going to hurt them?"

Her father's eyes flickered away from hers for a moment, and Rommy felt like someone had punched her in the stomach. She stared at her father with horror. "Why? Why would you hurt them?"

Hook reached out to her again, but she stepped away from him. "I didn't believe it, all the things Pan said about you. I told him he was wrong." She let out a bitter laugh. "He wasn't the one who was crazy. It was me for believing in you. Everything I thought I knew about you was a lie, not just what you did, but who you are."

Her father's head snapped back like she had slapped him. "It's not like that, Andromeda."

"Then what is it like, Father? What if one of those boys was your son? What if someone tied him up and was going to hurt him?"

Rommy watched as all the color drained from her father's face and he suddenly looked old and tired. "What did you say?" he asked, his voice hoarse.

Rommy hugged herself and turned away from him. "I can't believe I ever defended you," she said.

Hook turned her back to face him. "Andromeda, I will not hurt the boys, but I need to find out what they know about Pan and his plans. If I let them go,

Pan has no reason not to attack us. I want to get you to someplace safe before that happens."

"I can't go back to Chattingham's right now," Rommy said. "Can't you see that everything has changed?"

"It certainly has. I don't know if you can ever go back to Chattingham's," her father said, grimacing.

"What do you mean, not ever? I have to tell Francie what happened. She might be in terrible trouble because of me."

"Francie can take care of herself. You wouldn't be safe there. Now that Pan knows where you are, he'll keep trying to get to you to get to me. They won't be able to keep you safe there, and how would I ever explain the precautions they'd need to take?" He shook his head. "No, I must find a new place for you, somewhere not in London." He looked at Finn and the little boy. "But we'll discuss that later. Now, you must go back with Smee to my quarters."

Rommy scowled and crossed her arms. "I'm not going anywhere until you promise me on... on... on Mama's grave that you won't hurt Fi...the fellows there."

"You have my word," her father said. He came to stand in front of her and lifted her chin. "Look at me, Andromeda." Rommy reluctantly raised her eyes to his. "I will not hurt either of these boys, but you must trust me. I know you feel I lied to you, but you don't understand everything that is going on here." He smiled at her. "You are so like your mother, always concerned about others." He ran his hand over her hair.

Rommy stiffened. How many times had he told her she was just like her gentle, fragile mother? In a flash of intuition, Rommy realized this was why he tucked her away at Chattingham's. This was why he never told her the truth of who he was and what he did. This was why he came to visit her twice a year, putting on a show. He didn't think she could handle the truth. Because she was just like her mother.

"Go with Smee now. I'll come see you in a little while," her father was saying.

Time slowed for Rommy. Suddenly, she could see what her future would be like. Her father would hustle her away, hide her someplace else. She'd never find out the answers to all her questions. They'd never truly know each other. It didn't matter that he put her at Chattingham's, that he said he wanted her to be strong and modern. All he'd ever see when he looked at her was her mother.

Unless she did something that would make him see someone else.

29
THE RISK

R ommy's eyes fell on the dagger strapped to her father's side. She knew what she had to do. Stepping forward to hug him, she wrapped her arms around his waist. He pulled her closer, and she looked up at him. A gentle smile curled across his face.

"I'm not my mother," she said.

As she drew back from him, her hand snaked out and yanked the dagger from its jeweled scabbard.

Whirling away from her father and Smee, Rommy leapt to the boys. She sliced at the ropes that held them. They were rough and thick, but Hook's dagger was razor sharp. It took only a moment before the cords lay loose in the boys' laps.

Finn gaped up at her. She turned and faced her father and Smee who were both looking at her in paralyzed shock.

Glancing over her shoulder, she yelled, "Quit staring at me and get out of here!"

Finn scrambled to his feet and pulled the little boy up with him. "Go, Walter," he said, pushing the little boy's shoulder. Walter didn't need any more urging, and he leaped into the sky. Finn looked back at Rommy and grinned, ready to take off himself. Then his eyes went wide and he lunged toward her.

"Look out," Finn said.

Rommy whipped her head around, but it was too late. A pair of brown arms came around her and lifted her off her feet. A chuckle sounded in her ear. "Well, now, looks like this pirate princess is a chip off the old block and make no mistake about it!"

In horror, she saw that the giant with the red beard had seized Finn too.

Rommy tried to kick her captor whom she couldn't see, but he just laughed as if he hadn't had this much fun in ages. She tried to bite him, but he moved his hand before she could latch onto him. "Hey now, none of that. And here Stubbs was telling me what a lady you were. More like a spitfire."

"That enough, Max," said her father in a quiet voice. "Quit teasing her before she manages to get a bite out of you, and take that dagger away from her too before she stabs someone with it."

Max gripped her wrist and squeezed until she cried out and dropped the dagger onto the deck. Rommy stopped struggling and stared up at her father. His blue eyes met hers and then looked away. After a moment, he sighed heavily. "Red, bring the boy over here."

Rommy's stomach sank as the giant redheaded man brought a struggling Finn around to her father. Why hadn't he flown away when he had the chance? He'd tried to help her. Again. And look where that had gotten him.

She renewed her struggle. "Leave him alone," she said.

Her father ignored her completely. He used his hook to pull Finn's shirt until they were nose to nose. "Tell me what you know about Pan's plans, boy," said her father, his voice low and menacing. Finn just looked at him, so her father shook him. "I said, tell me what you know, boy, or even my daughter's pleas won't save your sorry life."

"Stop it, Papa! You said you wouldn't hurt him," Rommy said, squirming in Max's arms.

"Take her to my quarters, Max, and lock her in," her father said without taking his eyes off of Finn.

Max started to haul her away. "I'll get out," cried Rommy. "I'll get out, and I'll… I'll… I'll join Pan and become a Lost Boy."

Her father let go of Finn and was in her face so fast she gasped. "Don't threaten me, Daughter." She had never had that formidable anger directed at her. She now knew why the Lost Boys were afraid of Captain Hook. A small seed of fear unfurled in her belly, followed by a white hot anger that seared through her. How dare Papa make her afraid of him?

Max pulled her back a few steps. "Come on now, that's enough."

But Rommy wasn't finished. She narrowed her eyes at her father. "I hate you! Pan was right about you. You're nothing but a bloody pirate, and I wish I wasn't your daughter!" She spit the words.

A spasm of emotion flashed over her father's face and then was gone. He slowly straightened, and without a word, turned his back on her. "Take her away, Max," he said, with a wave of his hand. "And make sure you lock that door tight. Tell the men we'll be shipping out soon, as soon as I take care of this little matter." He nodded toward Finn.

30
THE PRISONER

Max carried her across the length of the deck to her father's quarters. A lump of tears felt stuck in her throat, but she swallowed them down. There was no way she would let any of her father's crew see her crying. She wasn't weak. She'd show them all. Rommy stopped struggling and held her head up high, chin out.

The pirate opened the door to her father's quarters and carried her into the room. When he set her on her feet, she whirled on him.

He laughed and held his hands out. "Easy now. There isn't any choice but to stay in here, so you might as well make yourself comfortable. Captain's got a terrible temper. I would advise you to stay out of his way for a while if you know what's good for you." He took in Rommy's furious expression.

"Although your temper might just be a match." He chuckled again as he headed out of the cabin.

He paused in the doorway. "You don't really hate him. It'll turn out all right. You'll see." Then he was gone, the lock clicking behind him. She rushed over to it, but the doorknob wouldn't turn. She spent a few fruitless moments tugging on it before admitting that she was stuck.

She hit the wooden surface witha strangled cry and then began to pace the room. Worry wormed into her thoughts. What would her father do with Finn? He said he wouldn't hurt Finn, but he threatened him. Surely, everyone wouldn't fear Captain Hook so much if he was just empty threats. Rommy kicked the door, frustrated at her helplessness. Her father could do something to Finn and tell her whatever he wanted. It was obvious his crew wouldn't go against him.

Back and forth Rommy strode, muttering to herself. She stopped now and then to put her ear to the door. Besides the basic clatter of people moving around doing whatever sailing things people did on a boat, nothing told her what was happening. She even stood on a chair to see out the porthole, but it looked out on the side of the ship. She could see nothing of interest from it.

To distract herself from all the worst case scenarios running through her head, she decided to explore her surroundings. The large trunk on the floor was locked, so she moved behind the screen. The bed was large, but that wasn't surprising. Her father was a big man, and she couldn't imagine him sleeping with his legs dangling off the end of the bed. Against the far wall of the cabin was a cabinet with drawers on the bottom and a series of cubby holes on the top.

Walking over, she opened the drawers, but clothing filled the space. Again, not a surprise. A small portrait of her and her father was tacked to the wall above the cabinet. She traced it with her finger, remembering when they had it made. Not this Christmas, but the one before. That was before her father had lost his hand, back when he was still someone she admired and respected.

She jerked her hand back. A lie, even that picture was a lie. She continued to look through the cubbies. One held a watch pin, like a woman would wear. She turned it over. Engraved on the back, it said, "My darling Camilla, all my love, James." Her mother's watch. If she had found this a week ago, Rommy wouldn't have hesitated to ask her papa if she could keep it, but now, well, now things were different. She placed it back where she had found it.

Another cubby held a small, carved car. She picked it up and turned it over in her hand. What an odd thing for her father to have. Maybe it was from his boyhood. When she put it back, her hand brushed against some paper. Curious, she tried to pull it out, but it was caught in the seam of the wood where two of the cubbies came together. She could see now it wasn't paper, but a photograph.

She continued tugging at it. Rommy didn't want to tear the picture, but her curiosity wouldn't let her quit. She ran her fingers along the seam and pulled again. The photograph finally came away, and she turned it over.

It was a picture of her father. A woman she presumed was her mother was sitting in front of him. Sitting in her lap was a chubby infant with a head of dark curls. Rommy stared at the photograph. She had always been told her mother died giving birth to her, but how could that be if someone took this picture? Had her father been married before Mama?

Rommy looked more carefully at the woman. The shape of her face, the curve of her mouth, the eyes - they were eerily similar to what she viewed in the mirror every morning. This had to be her mother, but why would her father tell her Mama had died in childbirth when she clearly hadn't? She squinted at the baby. She had certainly changed a lot. Was nothing her father told her true?

31

THE BATTLE

A great crashing noise made Rommy jump and drop the photograph. Something hit the door, hard.

Rommy hurried around the screen and ran to the door, pressing her ear against it. She could hear shouting and crashing and steel clanging against steel. Someone—probably Pan and his Lost Boys—was attacking the ship.

She pulled the chair over to the window and looked out. Again, there was nothing to see from this side of the cabin. Whatever was happening must be out on the main deck. She looked around the room and spotted a long quill pen lying by a stack of maps and charts. Snatching it up, she knelt in front of the door. She worked the pen into the small keyhole, but the tip was too thick to fit into the locking mechanism. She threw it to the floor and jumpd to her feet.

Rommy turned in a circle, looking for anything that would help her escape. Then noticed the window and an idea came to her. All she needed was something heavy enough to smash it. Her father would probably be angry, but at this point, did it really matter?

Rommy found what she was looking for on the table - a heavy paperweight. She began climbing onto the chair, but stopped and ran to the bed and pulled off a blanket. No use cutting herself to ribbons by flying glass.

Once more she climbed up on the chair. With one hand she held the blanket over the window. With the other, she reared back and hit the glass with all her might. A loud cracking sound filled the room. She hit it again, and the glass shattered, most of it flying outward onto the side deck.

Carefully, Rommy removed the blanket. There was a jagged fringe around the edge of the window. She took the paperweight and knocked off the glass edges. It wasn't easy, and some took a few tries, but eventually she got most of the bottom and sides cleared of any glass shards.

Rommy paused, and then, pushing off the chair, she floated up and out the window. She landed on the deck on the far side of the cabin; the sounds of the battle were deafening. She crouched against the cabin wall and crept closer to the main deck. Although the fighting was so loud, she probably could have worn clogs and danced her way onto the deck and nobody would have noticed. Rommy peered around the edge of the cabin, and her whole body went cold.

The entire deck was was swarming with bodies. It was impossible to tell who was who. And the noise. Steel rang against steel. Booted feet made for a macabre dance tune as the men and boys fought each other. Shouts and whooping war cries echoed out over the water. Boys were scrambling up the rigging and dropping onto the bigger pirates below to get the upper hand.

Rommy stared at the mass of bodies and stepped from the shelter of the cabin. Suddenly, she found herself flung against the front of the cabin wall, and a sword dug into the wood above her head with a thwack. Before she could see who had nearly decapitated her, a body was in front of her.

The clang of steel sounded loud in her ears as two bodies fought each other. She pressed herself up against the wall, trying to stay out of the way. The person in front of her fought his opponent toward the railing of the ship. With a mighty cry, he blocked the other man's blow and shoved. A body tumbled over the rail and there was a distant splash.

The boy turned around and Rommy realized it was Finn. He rushed over to her. "What are you doing out here? You need to get back in that cabin before you get yourself killed."

"Behind you!" Rommy screamed.

Finn whirled and blocked a blow from a tall pirate Rommy hadn't seen yet in her time on the ship. The man had dark hair pulled back in a queue and a dark tan from his time in the sun. He came at Finn with swing after swing, pushing Finn until he was against the cabin.

Rommy grabbed the sword still stuck into the wall and wrenched it from the wood. It was heavier than she was used to, but it was far better than the piece of wood she'd used in the alley.

The pirate was focused on Finn, so Rommy came around the side and stuck her foot out behind his leg. The pirate backed up to deliver a blow and tripped, falling against the railing. Finn rushed him and tipped him over into the water below.

Rommy peered over the rail. "I hope he can swim," she said.

Finn grabbed her hand and pulled her back around the side of the cabin. "I'm serious, Rommy," he said. "You need to go hide somewhere. These battles are so bloodthirsty, nobody will care if you're Hook's daughter, not even his own men. They'll skewer you before they even realize who you are. Hook will kill them for it, but it'll be too late for you."

Rommy lifted her chin. "I will not run and hide while everyone else is out here fighting. I can help."

"Help who exactly?" Finn asked. "Whose side are you even on?"

Rommy blinked at him. It was a good question. Pan was dangerous, she had no doubt, but her father didn't seem much better. She looked over at the battle still in full swing.

There were bodies lying on the deck, both big and small. She saw pools of something dark she didn't want to think about too much. Maybe Finn was right. Who would she even be fighting if she ran out there?

32

THE FACE-OFF

As Rommy looked out across the deck, the bodies parted and a path opened. She could see straight to the bow of the boat. Her father and Pan were locked into battle. Pan was darting in and out, but her father's longer sword gave him an advantage, even if he couldn't fly.

Pan attacked with brutal blows, but her father looked like he was dancing, his sword weaving in and out. She saw Pan pull back sharply and grab at his arm. Her father must have hit his mark.

Rommy would never know if she made some kind of noise or if her father just felt her eyes upon him, but he looked up. When he saw her, his eyes widened. His face lost all color.

Time ground to a halt as they locked eyes across the bloody deck. Sound receded and then came rushing back as Pan, seeing her father's distraction, attacked with vicious ferocity. He drove the captain back until he was against the great wheel of the ship. Pan's dirk flashed, slicing her father's arm and his sword clattered to the deck.

Rommy didn't wait any longer. She knew in that moment she didn't hate her father, and she would do anything to save him. Tightening her grip on her sword, she charged across the deck. Whether it was the fierce war cry that came ripping out of her throat or pure luck, she made it to the other end of the ship almost as if everyone moved out of her way.

Pan had her father pinned against the wheel. Her father had pulled his dagger, but he could barely raise his sword arm. He was forced use his hook which allowed Pan in too close. Rommy saw Pan's arm arc down toward her father's exposed throat and she sprang forward. Her sword clanged, stopping Pan's strike. The force of the blow reverberated up her arm. Pan gave a savage snarl. When he realized it was Rommy, his eyes widened. Then his mouth curved into a feral grin.

"Like father, like daughter," he said. "It looks like I can get rid of both of you at once."

"No!" her father cried, pushing himself away from the ship's wheel. "Get away from him, Andromeda. I can't lose you, too."

Pan let out a crow of laughter. Then he flew up and beckoned Rommy toward him. The two met midair with a clang of steel. Rommy had the advantage with her longer sword, but Pan was wickedly quick with his dirk. Their blades came together again and again, the sound a discordant song.

Fighting in the air differed from dueling on the ground. Rommy had to adjust, but she found the ability to move vertically helped her. Her size didn't seem to handicap her as much in the air. The sounds of the battle on deck receded as they soared higher. All she saw was Pan. All she knew was the next strike and counter attack. As it always did, time slowed down and she could almost see Pan's next move.

Rommy had the advantage over Pan. Her ability to match him in skill had surprised him. She used that surprise, attacking Pan with a flurry of strikes and lunges. The strength of her attack maneuvered Pan down and toward the fore mast.

"You can't win." His voice was shrill. "You can't beat me. You're a girl."

Rommy bared her own teeth in a savage grin. "But I'm not just a girl. I'm Hook's daughter."

Pan growled and lunged forward, swinging his dirk down.

Rommy blocked it with her sword. Pan used his leverage to bear down on her. His face was only inches away, eyes narrowed.

"They're not worth it, you know. Grown-ups, parents —they're all liars. You can't depend on any of them. Even your precious father."

"You're wrong," said Rommy, shoving him with all her strength.

Pan was forced back and retreated a few feet to regroup. "I'm not. They're the enemy."

His eyes shifted toward the deck and he smiled recklessly. "But it looks like at least one of the enemy is going to die."

Rommy couldn't help it. She turned her head away from Pan to look down at her father. Her moment of inattention was all Pan needed. His laugh made her whip her head back up, but it was almost too late. Pan swung his dirk and Rommy desperately danced out of the way, but the tip of his blade slashed across her arm. She cried out and almost dropped her sword, but at the last minute her training kicked in. She clenched her fist, barely keeping her grip.

Whatever advantage Rommy had vanished as she felt warm liquid trickle down her arm. Pan smiled showing all of his teeth.

"You don't have to die, Rommy," he said as the two circled each other high above the ship's deck. "You can join me and leave your worthless father behind." He sneered at her. "He won't even miss you."

"You're wrong, Pan, and I would never join you."

Pan shrugged. "Have it your way."

Then he rushed toward her, slashing at her, pushing her toward the mast. Rommy blocked each strike of his dirk, but her arm was on fire and weak, making her reactions slower.

She found her back hitting the rough wood of the mast. Pan filled her vision. She gripped her sword harder. Blood was now dripping off her hand, and it made the hilt slippery. She clenched her teeth against the pain. She would not lose to this vile boy.

Pan's dirk came down in a punishing blow. She blocked it with her sword, but just barely. Her arms shook with effort as he pushed down harder, using all of his weight for leverage. Rommy's arms bent under the strain.

Pan smiled, his eyes intent on her face. "Are you so sure he's worth your loyalty? No grown-up's worth dying for."

Rommy dug deep into the last of her reserves and took hold of her courage with both hands. It might not work, but it was her only chance. Taking a deep breath, she spun around and under Pan's outstretched arm striking him in the back. His own momentum working against him, he knocked into the mast. His grip on his dirk loosened, and he almost dropped it. Rommy's hand found his hair, and she pushed her sword tip into his back.

"My Papa's worth it."

Pan grunted. "He's still a liar."

"You're not such a truth-teller yourself, Pan. It's time to end this. Call off your Lost Boys."

"Or you'll what?" Pan spat at her. "You don't

have the guts to draw blood." He let out an ugly laugh.

Rommy pushed the point of her sword until it just broke the skin. Pan hissed in a breath.

"I'm more Hook's daughter than you think," said Rommy in a hard voice. "Drop your dirk and call them off."

Pan hesitated, and she tightened her grip on his hair, her sword tip biting a bit deeper. A small, dark stain spread on the back of his tunic.

Pan uncurled his hand from his dirk one finger at a time until it clattered to the deck below them. He brought his fingers to his lips and gave a shrill whistle. She watched as the bodies doing battle disengaged. The smaller ones dashed to the sides of the ship and slipped over the rails. Within a few moments, the deck had cleared and only her father's crew remained.

It was only then that Rommy realized her father had started to climb up the mast using his hook to pull himself upward. His injured arm was pulled into his side, and he clenched his dagger in his teeth. He was staring up at her and Pan, his face white and desperate. Their eyes met and Rommy thought she saw the sheen of tears.

Tearing her eyes away from her father, Rommy shoved Pan away from her and raised her sword in front of her. "Go on, get out of here. I'm showing you mercy, but the next time I won't."

Pan spun in midair and pointed his finger at her. "Why did you defend him? He lied to you and tricked you. He abandoned you."

Rommy shrugged. "I love him, and I know he loves me. Papa may not have been truthful, but he's never abandoned me, and I know he never will."

Pan laughed. "You're such a sap, and you'll pay for it. This isn't the end. I'll be back, and next time the ending will be different."

Rommy watched as Pan whirled and flew away.

33
THE REUNION

Rommy floated back down to the deck. Her arm burned, and she was a bit lightheaded. Before she could even check to see where her father was, she was in his arms. He had leapt to the deck and reached her side in one large stride.

"Rommy, my Rommy," he said, his voice catching on the nickname he hadn't used in years, as he kissed the top of her head. "How did you.. I mean.. I thought I would lose you, and you're hurt..." He set her away from him to inspect her arm. "You've a nasty cut," he said. "That vicious little brat."

"I'm all right, Papa," she said, and then smiled. "He really *is* a vicious brat."

Her father laughed and pulled her into his arms once more. "I had no idea you could wield a sword like that, darling. You were marvelous."

Rommy smiled against her father's chest and

pulled back to look up at him. "I've been fencing for a long time, Papa. I made the varsity team at Chattingham's. That was my big news for your visit… and then you never showed up."

"I can certainly see why you made the team. I'm so proud of you." He shook his head in wonder. "I had no idea."

"That's the point, Papa, you don't know me very well. How can you when you only see me a few times a year? And I certainly don't know you, do I?"

Hook blinked rapidly and he wiped at his eyes. "I think that needs to change," he said.

A burst of joy bloomed in Rommy's chest and a grin spread across her face. "Do you mean it, Papa? Can I stay with you for a while?"

Her father smiled. "I think we can at least spend this summer together. I mean it when I say I don't know if you can return to Chattingham's. If Pan knows where you are…"

Rommy looked down. She didn't want to tell her father it was really Finn who had found her, but if her father thought Pan knew where Chattingham's was, she'd never be able to tell Francie she was all right. "Pan wasn't the one who brought me here. He didn't even know I existed until, um, until Finn brought me here." She looked up at her father's exclamation. "I don't really think Finn likes Pan, though, Papa. He seems afraid for the Lost Boys." She slowly shook her head. "I don't think Pan treats them very well or cares much about them. He says he does, but he doesn't."

Her father's arm tightened around her. "No, he doesn't. Pan offers those boys up like so many sacrificial lambs." Hook gave a bitter laugh. "After all, he can always find more."

Rommy and Hook moved toward his quarters, each cradling an arm. "That's just it, Papa, I don't think he finds them. I think he takes them."

Hook stopped in his tracks and stared down at her. "What do you mean?"

Smee came bustling up alongside them. "Eh, Captain, you're hurt, and you too, little miss. Let's get you to your cabin, and I'll get you both fixed up right quick." Smee beamed down at Rommy. "And you, young lady, that was some fine fighting, some of the finest I've seen, and that's saying something."

As they crossed the deck, her father on one side and Smee on the other, the men let up a cheer. As they passed through the crew, Rommy heard snatches of what the men were saying. "Good fighting, lass." "The apple doesn't fall far from that tree." "A chip off the old block she is, no matter that she looks so sweet." "That'll teach old Pan."

She ducked her head in embarrassment. Her father just let out a booming laugh. "That's right," he bellowed at the men, "she's my daughter and don't you forget it."

The men let out another cheer. A few whistled

and stomped their feet. Rommy's face got hot, but she smiled at them, anyway.

As they made their way into the cabin, Hook fished something out of his front pocket and held it out to her. Her pearl necklace dangled in front of her. She held out a trembling hand and he gently laid it in her palm.

"I would put it on you, darling, but with this arm, I don't think I could fasten it." Hook lifted his injured arm.

Rommy smiled with quivering lips. "It's all right, Papa," she said as she fastened it around her own neck. She fingered the pearl, remembering when she had given it to Chief Hawkeye. Suddenly she gasped.

"Alice!" she exclaimed. "With everything going on, I almost forgot about her." She grabbed her father's good arm. "We have to go get her, Papa."

"Alice? Who is this Alice, may I ask?" Hook said as he sat in his chair in front of the stove, Rommy next to him.

Smee built up the fire and rolled out a set of tools. He laid out some thread and a pair of scissors. He knelt next to Rommy first and gently cut away her sleeve and inspected her wound. "Well, isn't that good news?" he said. "It's a bleeder, but it isn't deep at all." Smee clucked his tongue. "That nasty boy has caught you neatly all the way across the top of your little arm." Smee poured something out of a bottle onto a cloth, and his brow furrowed. "I'm sorry to say this is going to hurt like a bag of eels, but thanks be, I won't have to stitch you up, too."

Rommy's father held her other hand, and then Smee, with a worried look, put the cloth on her arm. She hissed in a breath as the cut crawled with fire. After a moment, he sat back and let out a deep breath. "There now, the worst is over," he said.

Smee rummaged around in his kit again and brought out one of the little pots of ointment and smeared it along the cut. The fire in her arm immediately cooled. Neatly, he wound a bandage over her wound. He got up and patted her shoulder. "Brave lass. Not a peep out of you, bless your heart."

Then he turned to Hook and shook his head.

"You'll not get off so easy, Captain," said Smee.

Hook shrugged out of his leather coat with a grimace. "Be sure you mend that tear in my coat sleeve when you're finished with my arm," he said. "I don't think the shirt can be saved." He reached up and ripped the sleeve off from the shoulder.

Rommy swallowed and looked away. Blood covered his upper arm, and she had seen muscle.

"Now, Captain, I'm going to have to clean this out," said Smee, an apology in his voice. "It will hurt like the dickens." He looked at Rommy. "You may want to step out, dear. It's not for the fainthearted."

Rommy stood up. "I'm not fainthearted." She

knelt in front of her father and gently took his hand. "Hold on to me, Papa. I won't let go."

Her father smiled down at her and squeezed her hand.

His eyes closed and Rommy could see him gritting his teeth as Smee poured the whisky over the wound. She could feel his arm ripple with the pain.

"I'm here, Papa," she said, holding his hand with both of hers. "I'm here and I won't leave."

34

THE NEW BEGINNING

When Smee was finally finished, her father's face was grey with pain, but a neat line of stitches closed up the ugly wound.

Smee gathered up his instruments and the bowl of bloody water. "There now, Captain, the worst is over," he said. "You just rest that arm and spend some time with your darling daughter. The crew will clean things up. I don't think we'll have any more trouble with Pan and his boys tonight."

Rommy got up from her kneeling position on the floor. Her right foot had gone to sleep and was now tingling with pins and needles. She limped over to the chair and drew it closer to her father.

"Are you all right?" she asked.

"I'm fine," he said. "This isn't the worst thing that's happened to me." He raised an eyebrow and held up his hook.

"That doesn't make me feel better," Rommy said, but she was smiling. Then her smile faded, and she bit her lip. "I'm sorry I said I hated you. I didn't really mean it."

He reached out his hook and gently touched her cheek. "I know you didn't. You may look like your mother, but I think you have a touch of my temper." He smiled. "Now who is this Alice and why is she your responsibility?"

"It's rather hard to explain," said Rommy. "When I was coming to find you, I was going to the docks to see if I could find anything at your offices." She rushed on when she saw the frown on her father's face. "On the way, I got lost, and I was passing this alley. These big boys were going to hurt this little girl, Alice. I couldn't just let that happen. I had to help her." Rommy looked up at her father to see if he understood.

"I know you don't want me to say this, but you remind me so much of your mother," he said. "I'm sorry I've given you the impression that she was weak, but she wasn't. Not in the ways that were important. Yes, she was delicate and her health was always fragile, but she also cared about the small and unprotected, just as you do. I wouldn't want you to lose that. It certainly doesn't mean you are weak."

Rommy blinked back sudden tears. "That's the most you've ever said about Mama," she said.

"That was a mistake on my part, but losing her

was very hard," said Hook, his voice a bit rough. He cleared his throat. "Now, where is this Alice?" He sat up straighter. "Please don't tell me that Pan has her."

"No, the Indians have her," said Rommy. "Little Owl and Chief Hawk Eye wouldn't let Pan take her. They didn't really want Pan to take me, but Chief Hawk Eye thought that maybe I was the only one that could help the Lost Boys." Rommy paused. She and her father were getting along, and she was almost afraid to say what she was thinking out loud. "They thought you would hurt the boys, and, well, it looked like they were right."

Hook sighed and looked down at his hand that was still holding one of hers. "Andromeda... Rommy, I know what you think, but I have never caused permanent harm to any of the Lost Boys. I'll admit, sometimes it is hard to not let the ends justify the means when it comes to catching Pan, but I wouldn't hurt those boys, not purposefully."

Rommy still felt unsure. "But on the ship, I saw them. There were..." she swallowed, "bodies and blood. You may not hurt those boys, but your men do."

"You don't understand, Rommy. This is an island of magic, but those men, they're pirates. They aren't pretending, and I can't keep them from doing what a pirate does, not if I want to keep command of this ship. I try hard to avoid the kinds of fights we had tonight, but Peter Pan is always looking for an excuse to cross swords."

Rommy frowned. "But why, Papa? Why do you want to stay here and catch Pan so badly? I mean, he's frightening and cruel. As Alice said, he's balmy in the crumpet."

A bark of laughter burst from her father's mouth. "Yes, he is balmy in the crumpet, and you were right. He doesn't care about those boys. He doesn't care what happens to them as long as he gets what he wants. That is reason enough to catch him."

Rommy leaned forward. "But why you, Papa? Why is catching him so important that you've abandoned our life together and lied all this time?"

"I didn't want to lie to you, Rommy." He ran a hand over his face. "It's a long, complicated story, but when I started all this you were barely toddling. When you were so young, I couldn't tell you about all this, and the time just never seemed right to break my silence." He leaned forward, his gaze intent on her face. "We had such little time together as it was; I knew any explanations would only give you more questions. Do you understand, Rommy? I didn't mean to deceive you. I just wanted you to be safe and happy."

Rommy nodded and looked him right in the eye, willing him to understand. "I can see how the lie grew, but you should have told me. I've been old enough to understand for a while now."

Her father shook his head, a smile playing around his mouth. "It was easier to just keep things as they were."

"Easier for who?" Rommy asked, pulling back. "I still don't understand why you must do this. It makes no sense to me. How do you even know all this exists, and why is it up to you to stop Pan?"

"That's a lot of questions, my dear. Too many after such a long day, but all you really need to know is that Pan took something precious from me, and I can never get it back. I can't rest until he pays for that."

Rommy saw tears in her father's eyes, her father who never cried. The photograph flicked through her mind, and a suspicion blossomed. "What did he take, Papa?"

Her father shook his head. "That is a long story and one for another day."

Rommy considered pushing back, insisting on an answer, but she could see her father's face was still grey. He looked so tired. She could have lost him today, so she let him change the subject.

"Let's get back to your little friend Alice," he said. "I think that if she is with the Indians, she faces no immediate danger. If she was running around the alleys of London, she's probably better off with them. They are good people and will take good care of her. Little Owl loves children. It's why they always side with the Lost Boys."

"That and you tried to drown Tiger Lily," Rommy said, raising an eyebrow.

"That was just a ploy," said Hook. "I hope you know that I wouldn't let a young woman drown, even if she is rather unpleasant." Her father grimaced and then patted her hand. "We'll go fetch Alice from Chief Hawk Eye tomorrow. It's really too late now."

Rommy pushed up from the chair and looked toward the porthole window. The sun had set long ago, and Rommy could make out the lavender moon and the pale pastel stars. She yawned.

Her father pulled himself out of the chair and came to stand behind her. He hugged her to him.

"I was so afraid I would lose you today, even as amazing as your fighting skills are," he said softly into her hair. "I don't know what I would have done if something had happened to you too."

She turned and wrapped her arms around his waist and hugged him back. "I don't plan on going anywhere, Papa. You can count on that."

Her father patted her on the back and straightened, wiping his hand across his eyes. "Enough of all this," he said a bit brusquely. "Why don't you wash up and climb into bed. It sounds like tomorrow will be a big day if we're to get your Alice. I'll be back in a little while to tuck you in. I've missed being able to do that."

Even though she had been too old to be tucked into bed for a while now, Rommy nodded. She watched as her father made his way to the door and then closed it behind him.

She stared at the door for a moment. She still didn't have all the answers to her questions, but she had her father. When she had come looking for him, she had never expected what she found. Papa wasn't who she had thought he was, but she had surprised him, too.

"It will be different this time," she said outloud. She looked around the empty cabin, a cabin that happened to be on a pirate ship. "This time I won't let you send me away. I'm staying right here, so we can really know each other."

Turning away from the door, Rommy got ready for bed. Tomorrow promised to be an interesting day, but then, she had a feeling that every day in Neverland was an interesting day.

W ant to share your favorite books and have fun, too? Sign up for my email list and get a free printable book club toolkit as a thank you. Once or twice a month you'll get updates on new releases, my favorite book recommendations, and fun goodies and contests that are only available to my newsletter subscribers. Visit here (or have a parent do it for you) to get started: http://eepurl.com/dKEPd-/

Or you can scan the QR code below.

~

WONDERING what happens to Alice and what Hook's Secret is? Don't miss *Pan's Secret: A Pirate Princess's Quest for Answers* to find out!

BE CAREFUL WHAT YOU WISH FOR.

When Andromeda "Rommy" Cavendish finally found her father, she thought it would be the best summer of her life. Even if her father really is a pirate named Captain Hook.

But she quickly finds out how wrong she is.

Between Pan's secret and her father's thirst for revenge, Rommy once again finds herself on a quest for answers. But this time, the journey leads Rommy and her friends into the heart of Neverland's terrifying jungles. They must find the only one who has the knowledge Rommy needs.

Unfortunately, she might not be talking.

If you enjoy fast-paced fantasy adventures with talking wolves, feisty heroines, and fairytale twists, you'll love *Pan's Secret: A Pirate Princess's Quest for Answers*, second in the middle-grade fantasy adventure trilogy the Pirate Princess Chronicles.

JOIN THE QUEST AND PICK UP YOUR COPY TODAY!

Made in USA - North Chelmsford, MA
1368092_9780578412450
04.24.2023 1353